BLUE

is the

COLOR

of

SEDUCTION

An Erotic Thriller
by

JULIET MᶜDUFF

For all those women in need ...
but be careful what you wish for.

1

Samantha's body glistened with a sheen of sweat as she moved atop Keith, her hips undulating sensually in the dimness of their bedroom. The light of early morning filtered through the curtains, casting everything in a dreamlike glow. Sam's breathy moans of pleasure mingled with the creak of the mattress springs and the soft rustling of rumpled sheets.

"Keith ..." she gasped, picking up the pace. Her fingernails dug into the muscles of his chest as ecstasy built within her. Keith grunted in response, his hands gripping her waist ...

But Sam recognized the distracted look in his eyes, as if his mind was already on the day ahead rather than caught up in the throes of passion with his wife.

With a few final mechanical thrusts, Keith shuddered his mild, always mild, release. Samantha kept grinding against him, desperate to reach her own climax, but the intensity she needed had passed. She bit back her frustration as Keith, oblivious as always, shifted out from under her.

"Sorry I can't cuddle, honey," he said, planting a quick peck on her forehead. "I've got to shower and get ready for work." And he padded off to the bathroom.

Sam flopped back against the pillows with a sigh, the ache between her legs unquenched. A hollow feeling settled in her chest as she listened to the hiss of the shower spray in the adjacent room. Tears pricked the corners of her eyes.

Another round of lovemaking, and still her womb probably remained empty, as they weren't getting any younger. At this rate, she feared she would never fulfill her deepest desire of becoming a mother. Keith expressed sympathy, but overall seemed as oblivious to her actual pain, content as he was with their comfortable suburban existence, as he was to her sexual dissatisfaction.

For Samantha, "contentment" wasn't enough — especially when a vital piece was missing. She craved more, a spark of excitement to liven up the monotony. And perhaps, God willing, the blessing of a child created from a union of true passion.

Rolling out of bed, Samantha slipped on her silk robe and went to make coffee, trying to shake off her melancholy before facing another day of household chores and listless hours spent alone.

Little did she know, the winds of change were about to blow her way from a most unexpected direction ...

* * *

The aroma of freshly brewed coffee filled the kitchen as Samantha sat at the table, gazing out the window at the perfect blue sky, so at odds with her inner turmoil. With Keith gone off to work and just her in the house, the ticking of the antique wall clock seemed unnaturally loud, counting off the seconds of yet another humdrum day.

As she sipped the hot, bitter-but-robust liquid, a flicker of movement in the corner of her eye caught her attention. She turned to see a large, glossy black raven perched on the sill, studying her with strangely intelligent eyes. Samantha felt an unexpected chill snake down her spine as the bird held her gaze, unblinking.

"Now where did you come from?" she asked. "Haven't seen any ravens your size before, not around here."

As abruptly as it appeared, the raven took flight, leaving behind a single iridescent feather on the ledge.

After a moment's hesitation, Samantha set down her coffee, rose, and went to open the window just enough to retrieve the feather. Rolling the soft plume between her fingers, she wondered at such an odd occurrence ... and yet, she felt inexplicably comforted, her troubles forgotten, however briefly, in the unique experience — shared with a bird, of all things.

Tucking the feather into the pocket of her robe, she finished off her coffee and started in on the day's typical tasks — laundry, vacuuming, scrubbing the sinks until they gleamed ... but her mind drifted back to the raven, a splash of the wild and untamed in her otherwise beige existence.

As she went through the motions of her daily routine, her thoughts refused to let go of the unexpected encounter with the raven. She couldn't shake the feeling that the bird's appearance held some deeper significance, like a sign from the universe itself. Absently dusting the shelves lined with Keith's chiropractic textbooks and the various knickknacks they'd collected over the years, she paused to study their wedding photo, a wistful sigh escaping her lips.

There they stood, frozen in time, bright-eyed with the promise of happily ever after. But reality had proven somewhat less idyllic than the fairy tale she'd once envisioned. Though she loved Keith, his even-keeled stability that had initially drawn her now felt more like a stifling cage of ... sameness. The spark between them was gradually but undeniably dimming, reducing to dying embers that barely sustained her.

Loading the dishwasher, Samantha found herself humming an old love song, one that conjured bittersweet memories of the early enthusiasm in their marriage. They used to dance together in the kitchen, swaying to the music as the sunset painted the room in shades of gold and pink. When she closed her eyes, she could almost feel Keith's arms around her, his breath warm against her neck as he held her close. But those carefree days seemed like a lifetime ago, lost to the tedium of the everyday.

Sam yearned for something more, an intangible whisper of excitement to rattle the too-steady rhythm of her days. Even her paintings, once a source of joy and creative outlet, had grown lackluster, as if the well of inspiration within her had run dry. She glanced at the half-finished canvas propped in the corner of the living room, the abstract swirls of color now appearing chaotic and meaningless.

Hours blurred together, the sun tracking its path across the sky, until the purr of Keith's car in the driveway announced his return. He greeted her with a distracted smile, already loosening his tie as he beelined for the den and the waiting television. Dinner was a silent affair, the only sounds the clink of silverware on plates and the droning of some sitcom laugh track from the next room.

Later, Samantha climbed into bed beside her already snoring husband and switched off the lamp.

<h1 style="text-align:center">2</h1>

The next morning dawned, grey and ordinary, mirroring the emptiness Samantha felt as she watched Keith drive off to work. Alone again in the too-quiet house, she went through the motions of her daily rituals — brewing coffee, tidying up, putting in a load of laundry. Each task blurred into the next, an endless cycle of domestic drudgery that left her soul parched and withering.

As she stood at the kitchen sink, absently scrubbing at a stubborn spot on a plate, a flash of movement outside the window caught her eye. Setting the dish down, she leaned forward to peer into the narrow alley that ran between their house and the neighbor's. There, she spied a man crouched down, his back to her. Curiosity piqued, she watched as he extended a hand toward a scrawny, feral-looking cat that paced warily just out of reach.

The stranger's movements were slow, non-threatening, his posture relaxed and patient. He murmured something Sam couldn't make out, but his deep, melodic voice weaved a spell of calm. Inch by tentative inch, the bedraggled feline crept closer, sniffing the air, until at last it nuzzled against the man's open palm.

A smile tugged at the corner of Samantha's

mouth, charmed by the unexpected scene.

As if sensing her gaze, the man glanced over his shoulder, and Sam found herself staring into a pair of striking blue eyes that pierced right through her. Waves of dark hair fell across his forehead, contrasting with the chiseled planes of his face. He looked to be in his late twenties, with a lean, muscular build evident even through the fabric of his plain red T-shirt and faded jeans.

For a moment, they simply regarded each other, the rest of the world falling away. Sam felt an unfamiliar flutter low in her belly, a spark of something dangerous and exhilarating. Then the man quirked a knowing grin, giving her a little two-fingered salute before rising smoothly to his feet. The cat, now twining around his ankles, meowed plaintively as he turned and sauntered off down the alley, vanishing from view.

Samantha released a breath she hadn't realized she'd been holding, her heart doing a funny little skip-step in her chest. Shaking her head, she tried to refocus on the task at hand, but her mind kept straying to the mysterious stranger and those mesmerizing eyes. Who was he? She'd never seen him around the neighborhood before. And what was he doing coaxing stray cats in the alley?

Putting away the last of the dishes, she couldn't resist another glimpse out the window, half-expecting (or maybe hoping?) to see him reappear. But the alley remained empty, neither the feral cat nor her mysterious tamer in sight.

Samantha wandered into the living room and sank

onto the sofa, her morning routine abandoned. Sunlight filtered through the gauzy curtains, pooling soft golden light around her. She pulled the raven's feather from her robe pocket, twirling it between her fingers as she mused on the strange encounter that had left her both rattled and intrigued.

As much as she wished to dismiss the man in the alley as just some newcomer or drifter, he lingered in her thoughts like a sweet, forbidden melody, looping insistently. There had been something captivating about him — how he'd coaxed the skittish creature with such ease, and then entranced Sam herself with little more than a backward glance.

Setting aside the feather, Sam picked up her phone and absentmindedly scrolled through social media, hoping for distraction but finding none. Her thoughts continued to spiral back to that unsettling yet thrilling moment their eyes locked. She wondered if she'd find the nerve to mention it to Keith, but knew he'd likely dismiss it as nothing of consequence. His world of careful predictability left little room for mysteries or what-ifs.

Restless energy sparked within her; she needed something to do, somewhere outside the confines of these walls where she could stop obsessing over blue eyes and phantom excitement.

With sudden determination, Samantha snatched up her handbag and keys. Maybe a visit to the gallery downtown would rekindle some small flicker of inspiration in the cooled embers of her artistic spirit.

The drive was a blur of unremarkable scenery and radio static she didn't bother correcting. When she arrived at the small art studio where she'd once shown a few pieces, there was an unfamiliar sense of vacancy. The owner (an effeminate heterosexual, if there ever was one) greeted her with polite disinterest — they hadn't seen any new work from her in months, after all — though he feigned enthusiasm while showing off his latest curated exhibits.

"You should think about submitting again," he said, with barely concealed indifference.

"Soon," Samantha replied with a hollow promise, glancing around at other artists' bold canvases that only deepened her sense of inadequacy. She thanked him and left before he could inquire too deeply into what had happened to stall her creativity.

Back home by early afternoon, Sam was surprised to see Keith's car, his early return unusual. Parking and approaching the door, she hesitated with her hand on the doorknob, willing herself to quell the flurry inside before facing him.

Inside, Keith was perched on their worn couch, tie undone around his neck like a noose hastily removed.

"Hey!" she said. "Didn't expect you back until later."

Keith's smile was warm but distracted, and Samantha felt an odd pang at how accustomed she had grown to its absence from his eyes.

He shrugged. "Figured I'd knock off early. Thought maybe we could go see a movie or grab dinner out?" Hopeful undercurrent beneath his words — did he somehow *finally* sense somehow that what held them together was starting to fray?

"Sure," Sam heard herself agree, though even as

she spoke it seemed distant from what tugged insistently at her heart. She didn't want a meal and movie, she wanted her husband to rush over here and ravish her!

Keith's gesture was sweet but felt obligatory, another attempt at kindling romance by following well-worn patterns: Dinner at their usual Italian spot; shared laughter that never quite reached his eyes across plates of predictable entrees; returning home to ... *maybe* ... engage in a humdrum round of rudimentary sex that left only him satisfied.

*   *   *

By the time they left for the restaurant, Sam's spirits had already dipped back into another melancholy haze. She forced herself to keep up appearances, feigning enjoyment through the courses and comfortable silences ... all the while grappling with the vivid memory of intense blue eyes and the cat-tamer's slow, knowing smile.

Back at home, Keith switched on sports highlights and cracked open a beer. Samantha eventually sauntered upstairs, slipping off her clothes and regarding her reflection in the mirror. She dropped the robe that clung to her curves into a silky puddle on the floor, wishing like hell that she could have distracted him from the game with her body. It was still a nice body, in her opinion; no, a *hot* body ... for all the good it did her.

Unconsummated desire sat heavy in her belly as she showered and climbed under clean sheets alone once again. She was tempted to masturbate, but what if Keith walked in on her? Would that embarrass him, or arouse him? She wished she could know.

But it was past midnight when Keith finally crawled in beside her. In minutes, Sam heard his soft snore rise and fall, and she stared at the darkened ceiling, restless and awake.

Tomorrow would be better, she told herself. An empty promise.

Or so it seemed until morning came.

3

A cat meowed outside their bedroom window; its sharp, early cries shredded Samantha's dreamscape. She awoke with a start to find Keith already gone, retailoring spines at his chiropractor office or drinking coffee at his desk while enjoying the contentment of an underwhelming life.

That's not fair, she scolded herself. *I need to watch the hostility. I can't help feeling like something is missing, but he can't help it if he doesn't.*

Samantha rose and padded through the still house to find herself drawn inexorably outside and around to that alley. The presence of feline sentry confirmed it: Rumpled black-and-white fur perched high atop slightly rusted trash can surveillance post. Waiting.

Bleary-eyed but heart skipping excited beat against flesh-rib cage — why did this stranger stir such longing inside her? — Sam stood beneath their bedroom window alongside the cat that had been left lonely by a brief whisper of departure.

She smelled him before she saw him.

Half-moons of sweat dampened his red T-shirt where it clung to skin shimmering bronze beneath morning haze. Hair fell ragged across his forehead, matching gait both loose-limbed and tightly wound all at once as he appeared around corner, breathing easy like he hadn't just run three blocks or three miles or three lifetimes toward her.

Samantha pretended not to notice his approach until he smiled in greeting.

"Morning," he said, his raspy voice cutting an easy, slow arc through air between them. It landed somewhere in the warmth of Samantha's chest.

Sam cleared her throat, uncharacteristic nerves latching onto her insides like tickling vines. "Morning," she echoed, the beautiful, enigmatic stranger now standing before her like an apparition manifested from thick ether of desire itself — six-foot-something, slight beginning-day stubble along his jaw line ... and that smell! Shouldn't a sweaty man stink? Not this fellow. Sam had never been a big "smeller," but this guy's scent did something to her nether regions ...

He reached out to the cat, stroking a gentle finger along its back. Then he extended his hand toward Samantha. "I'm Ty, Ty Boxx — with two Xs."

"Samantha Darby," she replied, taking his hand. The contact sent a jolt through her body, as if a current of electricity had found its way into her bloodstream. His hand was warm, calloused in places that spoke of manual labor, yet there was a gentleness to his grip that made her linger a moment too long.

"Nice to meet you, Samantha Darby," Ty said, holding her gaze with those impossibly blue eyes. They weren't just blue, she realized, but had flecks of something darker around the edges, like sapphires ringed with midnight. "I just moved into the house at the far end of the block. Inherited it from my uncle."

"Oh," Samantha said, suddenly aware she was standing outside in her thin silk robe, her hair uncombed, face bare of makeup. She fought the urge to cross her arms over her chest. "Well, uh ... welcome to the neighborhood, Ty."

The cat meowed, rubbing against Ty's leg with possessive insistence. He chuckled, a deep rumble that vibrated in the narrow space between them.

"This little guy's been keeping me company," Ty said, bending to scratch behind the cat's ears. "I think he's decided I'm his new person."

"Lucky cat," Samantha blurted, then felt heat rush to her cheeks. "I mean, most strays around here don't find homes so easily."

Ty's lips curved into a knowing smile, as if he'd heard everything she *hadn't* said. "I've always had a way with creatures that need something." His gaze flickered over her, brief but thorough. "Are you an artist, Samantha?"

The question caught her off guard. "I— wait, how did you—?"

"Your hands." He gestured. "There's a smudge of paint on your wrist. Deep blue, like the sky at dusk."

Samantha glanced down, surprised to find he was right. A small streak of ultramarine clung to her skin, a remnant from her half-hearted attempt to work on her abandoned canvas the previous evening after Keith had fallen asleep. She'd failed to wash it off, apparently.

"I used to be," she admitted. "Lately, I've been ... struggling with inspiration."

"A shame," Ty murmured, stepping closer. The

scent of him intensified—earthy and masculine with an underlying note she couldn't identify, something almost metallic. "I'd love to see your work sometime."

There was a weight to his words that made Samantha's pulse quicken. The morning air now felt too thick to breathe properly.

"I should get inside," she said, though every cell in her body screamed in protest. "Nice meeting you, Ty."

"The pleasure was mine, Samantha Darby—"

"Sam," she corrected.

He smiled, tilting his head slightly, those eyes never leaving hers. " 'Sam,' then. I'm sure we'll be seeing more of each other, Sam."

It sounded like just a pleasantry, but something told her it was more than that.

But then Ty nodded, turned, and walked away.

Back inside her house, Samantha paced restlessly from room to room. The encounter with Ty had left her skin humming with an electric awareness she hadn't felt in years. She tried to busy herself with mundane tasks — wiping down countertops, organizing the mail — but her mind kept circling back to those blue-sapphire eyes, that knowing smile, the intoxicating scent of him ...

By afternoon, she'd given up on productivity entirely. Sam settled onto the living room couch with a novel she'd been meaning to finish for months, hoping to lose herself in someone else's story rather than dwelling on the dangerous temptation of her new neighbor. But the words swam before her eyes, refusing to coalesce into meaning. She realized she'd read the same paragraph four times without absorbing a single sentence.

With a frustrated sigh, she tossed the book aside and leaned her head back against the cushions, closing her eyes ...

Immediately, Ty's face materialized in her mind—not as he had appeared this morning, but closer, his lips hovering just inches from hers.

In her imagination, his hands — those strong, capable hands — slid beneath her robe to caress the curve of her waist. Sam's breath quickened as the fantasy took hold. She could almost feel the heat of his body pressing against hers, pinning her against the alley wall where anyone might see them.

I've wanted you since I first saw you watching me, fantasy-Ty whispered against her neck, his breath hot on her skin. His fingers traced a path upward, grazing the underside of her breast with exquisite slowness.

Sam's hand moved unconsciously to her chest, mimicking the touch she craved. In her mind, Ty's mouth claimed hers in a hungry kiss that obliterated all thought of propriety or marriage vows. His tongue slipped between her parted lips as his thigh pressed between her legs, creating a delicious friction against her most sensitive spot.

Tell me what you need, he commanded, voice rough with desire.

"You," she gasped, both in fantasy and reality. "I need you, inside me."

Fantasy-Ty growled his approval, hitching her leg around his waist as he freed himself from his jeans. In one powerful thrust, he—

The sharp ring of the telephone shattered the illusion. Samantha's eyes flew open, her body flushed and trembling on the edge of release. Disoriented, she fumbled for the phone on the side table, struggling to regulate her breathing.

"H-Hello?" Her voice sounded strained even to her own ears.

"Hey, honey." Keith's familiar tones, cheerful and oblivious. "Just checking if we need anything from the store. I'm thinking of picking up steaks for dinner."

Guilt crashed over her like a wave of ice water. "Um, sure. Yes, that, uh ... that sounds good. Nothing else. Thanks."

"You okay? You sound weird."

"*Fine.* Just ... just fine."

Keith paused, for just a moment, then said, "Okie-dokie. Steaks for dinner. See you!"

After hanging up, Samantha pressed her thighs together, the ache between them still insistent. What was happening to her? She'd never been unfaithful to Keith, not even in her private fantasies. Yet here she was, practically writhing on their couch, imagining another man's touch while her husband shopped for their dinner.

She pushed herself up from the couch, legs unsteady beneath her. A cold shower — that's what she needed to clear her head.

As the icy water cascaded over her feverish skin, Sam tried to rationalize her reaction to Ty. It was natural, wasn't it? To be attracted to an attractive man? It didn't have to mean anything. Just a harmless fantasy to spice up her stagnant life!

... but even as she repeated these reassurances, something deeper whispered that there was more to it than simple attraction. Something about Ty felt ... *different*. Almost otherworldly. The way his eyes seemed to see right through her, the strange metallic undertone to his scent, how easily he'd tamed that feral cat ...

By the time Keith returned home, Samantha had composed herself. She smiled and kissed his cheek, playing the part of the dutiful wife while her mind wandered to blue eyes and strong hands. They ate their steaks on the patio, Keith chattering about a difficult patient he'd managed to help that day. Sam nodded at appropriate intervals, willing herself to be present, to be grateful for this comfortable life they'd built together.

That night, as Keith's familiar weight settled beside her in bed, Samantha stared into the darkness, wondering what Ty was doing just a few houses away. Was he thinking of her, too?

Sleep, when it finally came, brought dreams she would never admit to her husband.

4

Early the next morning, Samantha found herself drawn to her neglected easel. With trembling fingers, she squeezed fresh paint onto her palette—vibrant blues that reminded her of Ty's eyes, deep reds like his T-shirt, rich earth tones that evoked his skin. Without consciously planning it, she began painting a figure — muscular, powerful, its face obscured in shadow but its posture unmistakably masculine.

Hours slipped by unnoticed as she worked, her brush moving with a surety she hadn't felt in months. When she finally stepped back to assess her creation, her breath caught. Though she hadn't intended it, the painting was clearly of Ty — not a portrait exactly, but an impression of him, half-emerged from swirling darkness, hand extended toward the viewer in invitation.

"What am I doing?" she whispered, dropping her brush with a clatter.

Stomping into her bedroom in a frustrated huff, she flung herself onto the unmade bed. Staring up at the ceiling, the ache between her thighs had returned with vengeance, demanding attention she could no longer deny. She glanced at the clock — 10:17 AM. The day stretched before her, empty and waiting to be filled.

With a decisive movement, she untucked her shirt and slid her hand downward, trailing her fingers along her stomach toward her pubis. Her skin felt hypersensitive, as though every nerve ending had been awakened from a long slumber. She closed her eyes, allowing Ty's image to materialize in her mind — those piercing eyes, the knowing curve of his lips, the way his muscles had shifted beneath his T-shirt ...

Her fingers slipped lower, finding the slick evidence of her arousal. A soft gasp escaped her lips as she began to circle her most sensitive spot, pleasure spiraling outward from her core. In her mind, it was Ty's fingers exploring her, Ty's breath hot against her neck, Ty's weight pressing her into the mattress.

"Yes," she whispered into the empty room, her hips rising to meet her own touch. She increased the pressure, the rhythm, as fantasy-Ty whispered filthy encouragements in her ear.

The tension built within her, a gathering storm of sensation that made her breath come in shallow pants. She was close, so close—

"Cum for me, Sam," fantasy-Ty commanded, his voice rough with desire.

Her back arched as the orgasm crashed through her, wave after powerful wave of pleasure that left her trembling and gasping. Stars burst behind her eyelids as her body convulsed with an intensity she hadn't experienced in years, perhaps ever. For endless moments, she rode the crest of ecstasy, every muscle taut with release.

As the aftershocks subsided, Samantha lay boneless against the sheets, her chest heaving. A thin sheen of sweat covered her body, cooling rapidly in the morning air. She felt … freer. Lighter somehow, as though a weight she hadn't known she carried had been lifted. Her mind was blissfully empty of the restless thoughts that had plagued her for weeks.

The doorbell rang, its chime slicing through her post-orgasmic haze.

Sam froze, her eyes flying open. Who could be at the door at this time? The neighborhood was quiet during weekdays, most residents off at work or school.

The doorbell rang again.

Wiping her embarrassingly wet hand on the thigh of her jeans, Samantha hurried to answer it, her heart inexplicably racing …

… and when she pulled open the door, Ty stood on her threshold, the late-morning sun creating a halo around his head.

"Ty," she breathed, suddenly conscious of her flushed cheeks and disheveled appearance. The evidence of what she'd just been doing felt branded across her face.

"Morning, Sam." His voice was like warm honey, flowing over her sensitized skin. "Hope I'm not interrupting anything?"

There was something in his tone, a knowing lilt that made her wonder if he somehow knew *exactly* what he'd interrupted. Impossible, of course, but the thought sent a fresh wave of heat coursing through her body.

"No, not at all," she lied, one hand unconsciously rising to smooth her tousled hair. "What, um, what brings you by?"

Ty held up a small package wrapped in brown paper. "Found this on your lawn. Looks important, thought I'd bring it up to you." His eyes never left hers as he extended the parcel, forcing her to step closer to accept it.

The scent of him hit her again—that intoxicating blend of earth and musk and something metallic that made her nostrils flare and her pulse quicken. She took the package, her fingers brushing against his. Even that fleeting contact sent electricity skittering across her skin.

"Thank you," she managed, looking down at the unmarked parcel. "That's ... that's very neighborly of you."

Ty leaned against her doorframe, his posture casual, yet somehow predatory. "I believe in being a good neighbor, Sam. Helping out when someone needs ... something."

The weight he placed on that last word made her knees weaken. She found herself gripping the door handle for support.

"Would you like to come in?" The invitation slipped out before she could stop it. "For coffee, I mean."

Something flickered in those blue depths — triumph? amusement? — before his face settled into a smile that somehow did not quite reach his eyes. "I'd love that."

Samantha stepped back, allowing him to enter her home. As he passed, his shoulder brushed against hers, and she caught her breath at the contact. She closed the door behind him with a soft click that felt somehow final, like the sound of a trap springing shut.

"Nice place," Ty commented, his gaze sweeping the living room before landing on her easel in the corner. The painting she'd been working on was still there, uncovered — her interpretation of him emerging from shadow. "Is that new?"

Heat flooded her face. "I, uh ... yes. Just something I was experimenting with this morning."

Ty moved toward it with fluid grace, studying the canvas with an intensity that made her want to snatch it away and hide it. "Interesting choice of subject," he murmured. "You've captured something ... essential."

"It's not really of anyone specific," she lied again, the words sticking in her throat.

He turned to her then, one eyebrow raised in challenge. "No? Seems familiar somehow."

Samantha opened her mouth to deny any such possibility ... but no words came out.

Ty stepped closer to her. "Sometimes it's best not to say anything. Isn't it?"

Aware that her mouth was still hanging open, Sam shook her head, but her gesture of denial felt weak even to her.

Ty stepped toward her again, the distance between them almost gone. He whispered something, but in her flush of forbidden excitement, she couldn't make out what it was. For all she knew, it wasn't even English.

In that moment, she could not have cared less.

In one swift motion, Ty closed the remaining space between them and encircled her waist in his powerful arms. Before Sam could draw another breath, he lifted her effortlessly against his chest, one arm supporting her back, the other cradled beneath her knees.

"I've been watching you, Samantha Darby," he whispered, his lips grazing her earlobe as he carried her through her own home with unerring certainty. "Feeling your want. Your *need*."

Sam's head fell back, a moan escaping her lips as his mouth traced a burning path down her neck. She should protest, should tell him to stop, to put her down ... but the words dissolved before they could form. Instead, her arms wound around his neck, pulling him closer as he shouldered open her bedroom door.

He laid her on the rumpled sheets, still warm from her earlier pleasure, the scent of her arousal lingering in the air. Ty inhaled deeply, his eyes darkening to a midnight blue that seemed almost to glow.

"Your husband doesn't satisfy you," he stated, not a question but a simple truth as he loomed over her. "Let me show you what real desire feels like."

His mouth claimed hers in a kiss that obliterated thought. This was nothing like Keith's perfunctory pecks — this was devouring, consuming, a clash of tongues and teeth that sent liquid heat coursing through her veins. His hands were everywhere at once, tearing at her clothes with an urgency that matched the inferno building inside her.

Sam arched against him as he stripped away the last barriers between them, her fingers fumbling with the buttons of his jeans. When she finally freed him, the size and heat of him made her gasp. He was magnificent, perfect, impossibly hard against her palm.

"Please," she whimpered, shame forgotten in the face of overwhelming need. "I want you inside me. Now."

Ty's answering smile was feral, predatory. "Not yet."

He slid down her body, spreading her thighs with strong hands. The first stroke of his tongue against her center — still sensitive from her masturbation — had her crying out, hips bucking wildly. His grip tightened, holding her in place as he feasted on her with inhuman skill, bringing her to the edge again and again only to back away before she could fall.

"Ty!" she sobbed, fingers tangled in his dark hair. "Please, I can't— I need—"

"Tell me what you need," he commanded, echoing her earlier fantasy so perfectly it sent a shiver down her spine.

"You," she gasped. "Inside me. Now."

In one powerful thrust, he filled her completely, stretching her almost to the point of pain. Sam's nails raked down his back as he began to move, setting a punishing rhythm that had her seeing stars with each impact of his hips against hers.

"Look at me," Ty growled, his voice resonating with something inhuman beneath the surface. "Look at me as I take you."

Samantha's eyes flew open, meeting his gaze. For an instant, she thought she saw something flicker in those blue depths — a vertical slit like a reptile's pupil

— but it was gone so quickly, she dismissed it as a trick of the light.

His thrusts deepened, angled perfectly to hit that spot inside her that Keith had never found. The pleasure was almost unbearable, building to heights she'd never imagined physically possible. Every nerve ending in her body sang with sensation, her skin hypersensitive to his touch.

"You were made for this," Ty whispered, his breath hot against her ear. "Made for *me*."

He flipped her suddenly, pulling her up onto her hands and knees without breaking their connection. His hands gripped her hips with bruising force as he drove into her from behind, each thrust pushing her closer to some precipice she both feared and craved.

"I'm going to ruin you for anyone else," he promised, his voice thick with dark intent. "After today, nobody else — not your husband, *nobody* — will be enough. Only *me*."

One hand snaked around to find her center, circling with devastating precision. The dual assault — his thickness stretching her inside while his fingers worked their magic outside — had Sam keening, incoherent pleas falling from her lips.

"Yes," she sobbed, "yes, yes, yes!"

The room spun around her, colors intensifying, sounds amplifying. She could hear her own heartbeat thundering in her ears, feel every drop of sweat sliding down her spine. Ty's movements became frenzied, almost violent in their intensity.

"Now," he commanded. "Cum for me, Sam. Cum *now*."

The orgasm crashed through her like a tidal wave, obliterating everything in its path. Her body convulsed, muscles clenching so hard she thought she might shatter. Wave after wave of pleasure coursed through her, each more powerful than the last.

Dimly, she was aware of Ty's growl of completion, of something hot flooding her insides, of his body shuddering against hers. But these sensations were distant, secondary to the overwhelming ecstasy that consumed her.

Stars burst behind her eyelids, bright pinpricks of light expanding until they merged into a blinding white void. The pleasure was too much, too intense — her mind couldn't contain it. As the final, most powerful surge hit her, Samantha felt herself slipping away, falling into that white void, her body going limp beneath Ty's still-moving form.

Her last coherent thought was that nothing would ever be the same again.

5

When Samantha came to, the room was bathed in the golden light of late afternoon. She blinked, disoriented, her body feeling oddly weightless, yet achingly sore. For a moment, she couldn't process where she was ...

Then she remembered. She remembered the most amazing sex of her life.

She sat up slowly, sheets falling away from her naked form. Had she passed out? She must have, the intensity of their coupling overwhelming her senses completely.

And then Ty just ... left?

Sam stretched, wincing at the delicious soreness between her thighs. As she shifted, she noticed a wet sensation. Something was leaking from her — not unusual after sex without protection (a realization that should have horrified her, but somehow didn't).

Glancing down, she froze.

There, on the pristine white sheet between her legs, was a small puddle of fluid that had seeped from her body. But it wasn't the pearly white substance she was accustomed to seeing. This semen was ... *bluish*. A pale, ethereal bluish that seemed to shimmer slightly in the afternoon light.

"What the hell?" she whispered, touching it with

trembling fingers. It felt like normal semen — slick, slightly viscous — but such color was foreign to her. A faint metallic scent rose from it, reminding her of the strange undertone to Ty's natural musk.

Sam's heart began to pound. This wasn't normal. This wasn't possible. Men's semen wasn't any shade of blue, however subtle. She'd never heard of any condition or disease that would cause such a thing. A chill crept up her spine as she stared at the substance.

She yearned to question Ty about it. But of course, he wasn't there.

Then it struck her: What *time* was it?

A quick glance at the clock calmed her, somewhat; Keith shouldn't be home for at least another hour or more.

Except he came home early yesterday, didn't he?

Suddenly desperate to erase all evidence of her wild tryst, she stripped the sheets from the bed, bundling them into a tight ball. The bathroom mirror reflected her wild eyes and kiss-bruised lips as she shoved the sheets into the hamper. She turned on the shower as hot as she could stand it and stepped under the spray, scrubbing between her legs with almost frantic intensity.

Blue. Ty's semen was bluish. What did that mean? Was he sick? Was she now infected with something? Or was it something else entirely?

As she dried off, Sam's rational mind asserted itself through the panic. She needed information. Her laptop sat on the desk in the corner of the bedroom, and she wrapped herself in a robe before sitting down to search.

"Blue-tinted semen," she typed, then hesitated before hitting Enter. What if Keith somehow saw her search history? But she had to know. She pressed the key.

The results were disappointing — medical conditions that could tinge semen slightly yellow or green, but nothing about blue. Certainly nothing about the clear, almost luminescent cerulean shade she'd witnessed.

Sam closed the laptop, her thoughts spinning. The memory of Ty's eyes, his blue eyes, flashed in her mind. She vaguely remembered something about them during the act, something ...

Then she heard the front door open, and Keith call out in greeting.

Her husband was home.

"Hi, honey," Sam called back, frantically tying her robe tighter. She took a deep breath, willing her racing heart to slow. "I'm just ... getting out of the shower!"

"Perfect timing," Keith replied, his footsteps approaching the stairs. "I brought Chinese. Thought we could have a quiet night in."

Sam smoothed her damp hair, pinching her cheeks to bring color to them that wouldn't betray her afternoon activities. "Sounds wonderful," she managed, her voice steadier than she felt.

Throughout dinner, Sam maintained a façade of normalcy, laughing at Keith's anecdotes about difficult patients, asking appropriate questions, and even managing to eat despite the storm of confusion raging inside her. The blue-tinted semen, Ty's unceremonious disappearance, the intensity of their coupling — all of it swirled in her mind while she pretended nothing had changed.

"You're quiet tonight," Keith observed, setting down his chopsticks.

Sam forced a smile. "Just tired. I was painting today, got lost in it."

"That's great!" Keith's face brightened. "I've been hoping you'd get back to your art. Can I see?"

A flash of panic — the painting of Ty! "It's not ready yet."

Keith nodded, accepting her explanation without question, as he always did. His unquestioning trust only deepened her guilt.

After dinner, they settled on the couch to watch a movie. Keith's arm draped casually around her shoulders, the familiar weight both comforting and suffocating. Sam stared at the screen without seeing, her mind replaying every moment with Ty, every sensation, every inexplicable detail ... all sullied somewhat by the question of his bluish semen.

Halfway through the film, Keith's hand began to wander, stroking her arm, then brushing against the side of her breast. Sam tensed, not with anticipation but apprehension. When he leaned in to kiss her neck, she forced herself to tilt her head, giving him better access.

"Let's go upstairs," he whispered against her skin.

Now? she wanted to demand. *Damn it,* now *you decide to initiate things?!*

In their bedroom, with fresh sheets hastily applied before dinner, Keith undressed her slowly, methodically — so different from Ty's urgent, almost feral disrobing. His kisses were gentle, familiar, lacking the consuming fire that had burned through her earlier. Yet Sam found herself responding, relieved that Keith wanted her, that perhaps their connection wasn't as fragile as she'd feared.

When he finally entered her, Sam barely suppressed a wince. She was tender, the aftermath of Ty's vigorous possession making itself known. Keith, eyes closed in concentration, didn't notice her discomfort. His movements were predictable, the rhythm one she knew by heart after years of marriage.

"You feel amazing," Keith murmured, his pace increasing slightly. "You are amazing."

Sam made appreciative noises, her hands running along his back, trying to lose herself in the moment. But there was no disguising the truth: After Ty, Keith's touch felt muted, like watching an old black-and-white film after experiencing vibrant Technicolor. Sam closed her eyes, summoning images of Ty to help her through, guilt gnawing at her even as pleasure built.

When Keith reached his climax with a gentle shudder, Sam faked her own, moaning softly and arching beneath him. He collapsed beside her, pulling her close with a contented sigh.

"I've missed this recently," he whispered, kissing her temple. "We should make more time for each other, together. Not just ... you know, watching movies and stuff ... we should take ... take a little holiday ... or something ..."

Sam nodded against his chest, unable to form

words around the lump in her throat.

Within minutes, Keith's breathing deepened into sleep, while she lay wide awake, her body unsatisfied, her mind racing.

What had she done? Who *is* Ty Boxx, really?

And most disturbingly, why did she already crave him again, despite everything?

6

Dawn found Samantha in the kitchen, on her third cup of coffee, dark circles shadowing her eyes. She'd barely slept, plagued by strange dreams where Ty watched her from the shadows, his eyes glowing with an unearthly blue light.

Keith came downstairs, expressing surprise at her early morning. But even he soon had to leave for an early appointment, kissing her goodbye with renewed affection. His parting words — "Love you, beautiful"— had lodged in her chest like shards of glass.

The sound of something scratching at the back door pulled her from her gloomy thoughts. Cautiously approaching, Sam peered through the glass panel to see the same feral cat from yesterday, sitting expectantly on her doorstep.

"Well, hello to you again," she murmured, opening the door a crack. The cat meowed, its yellow eyes fixed on her face with surprising intelligence.

Before she could stop it, the creature darted between her legs and into the house. Instead of exploring as most cats would, it sat in the center of her kitchen floor, tail curled neatly around its paws, watching her.

"I don't have any cat food," Sam told it, feeling

slightly ridiculous for explaining herself to a stray.

The cat continued to stare, unblinking.

Then it stood, stretched languidly, and padded toward the living room with purpose. Curious despite herself, Sam followed. The cat stopped before her painting of Ty, looking back at her with what seemed like expectation.

"What do you want, exactly?" she asked.

The cat meowed once, then turned and trotted to the front door, clawing at it insistently.

"You want out now? Make up your mind." Sam moved to open the door for it, but froze when she saw a figure through the peephole.

Ty stood on her porch, hand raised to knock.

Her heart hammered against her ribs. Part of her wanted to pretend she wasn't home, to hide from the complications he represented. But when he knocked, a stronger impulse propelled her forward, her hand moving of its own accord to open the door.

"Morning, Sam," Ty said, his voice low and intimate, as if they shared a thousand secrets. Which, in a way, they now did.

"Ty." His name emerged as barely more than a whisper. "I ... wasn't expecting you. Again. So soon."

His smile was slow, predatory. "Weren't you? Your little friend seems to think otherwise." He nodded toward the cat, which had slipped between her legs again to wind around his ankles, purring loudly.

"The cat?" She shook her head. "It just showed up a few minutes ago."

"Did it?" Ty crouched to stroke the creature, his powerful body folding with effortless grace.

"Interesting timing."

Sam's mouth went dry as she watched his long fingers caress the cat's fur. Those same fingers had explored her body yesterday, bringing her to heights she'd never imagined possible. The memory sent a flush of heat through her core.

"We need to talk," she said, struggling to keep her voice steady. "About ... yesterday."

Ty straightened, his blue eyes darkening slightly. "Sure. May I come in?"

She hesitated, acutely aware of the threat he represented — to her marriage, if nothing else. But she stepped aside anyway, allowing him to enter her home once again.

While the door was still open, the cat darted outside, disappearing from sight.

"Would you like some coffee?" Sam asked, desperate for something normal to do, some routine to cling to.

Ty shrugged, moving to the center of her living room. He turned to face her, arms crossed over his chest. The posture emphasized the breadth of his shoulders, the lean strength of him. "You wanted to talk, Sam. Go ahead."

Direct. Commanding. So unlike Keith's gentle deference. Sam took a deep breath, steeling herself. She supposed she should talk about this ... affair? Was that the right word? But something else — something more specific — had been nagging at her.

"Your ... when we ..." She faltered, embarrassed despite everything they'd shared, everything they'd done. "Afterward, I noticed something. The fluid you left inside me. Instead of being just, you know, a normal off-white, yours had a ... a bluish tint to it."

"Ah." He shrugged. "Sorry. I suppose I should have mentioned that — not that we did a whole lot of talking, did we?"

Samantha blushed further, but refused to look away as she nodded her agreement.

"I have a medical condition," he explained. "Don't worry, it's harmless — to you, anyway. It's a very rare form of Cyanosis."

Cyanosis, she repeated in her mind, committing it to memory for later.

"It has to do with my blood-oxygen," he continued. "Sometimes, when I get worked up ..." He smiled at that, and seemed to enjoy watching her squirm a little. "... my lungs don't do their job properly. Most people get a bluish color around their lips, or their nail beds, or sometimes over their whole skin. It's a sign of not enough oxygen circulating. The good news is, my rare version of Cyanosis means it's less dangerous to me than to most people. The odd news is, instead of turning my lips blue, it affects my semen. It comes out much lower on oxygen — which means I also have an exceptionally low sperm-count." He smiled again. "So, just in case you were worried about our lack of using protection yesterday, it's very unlikely that I could get you pregnant — *especially* when my cum is blue."

"But—" Sam began, a dozen more questions tumbling through her mind. How rare was this condition exactly? And why did it feel like there was something more he wasn't telling her?

Before she could voice any of these thoughts, Ty took two swift strides forward, standing right in front of her. His hand cupped the back of her neck, drawing her toward him with gentle but insistent pressure.

"Enough talk," he murmured, his breath warm against her lips. "I didn't come here for a medical consultation. And since your husband left early this morning, I want to take advantage of that. Don't you?"

His mouth claimed hers with devastating thoroughness, tongue sweeping past her parted lips to tangle with her own. The kiss was hungry, demanding, stealing her breath and scattering her thoughts like autumn leaves in a gale. His hands slid down her back to cup her bottom, lifting her against the hard plane of his body.

Sam moaned into his mouth, her questions evaporating in the heat of renewed desire. She should stop this — Keith had *just* left, for God's sake — but her body had other ideas, arching instinctively into his touch.

Ty broke the kiss, his eyes now a darker blue, almost midnight. "I've been thinking about you all night," he whispered, his voice a rough caress against her skin as his lips traced a path down her neck. "About how good you taste. About how you feel wrapped around me."

His hands slipped beneath her robe, finding her naked beneath. A growl of approval rumbled from his chest as his fingers explored her curves, relearning territory he'd claimed just yesterday.

"I wonder," he said, his tone deceptively casual as

he guided her backward until her legs hit the couch, "if you've thought about tasting me?"

Sam's breath hitched as he pressed gently on her shoulders, urging her to sit. She sank onto the cushions, eye level with the obvious bulge in his jeans. Her mouth watered inexplicably.

"I want to feel those pretty lips wrapped around me," Ty continued, his thumb tracing the outline of her mouth. "I want to watch you take me in, see how much of me you can handle."

The crude words should have offended her. Instead, they sent a fresh wave of heat pooling between her thighs. Sam found herself nodding, her hands already reaching for his belt buckle.

"That's it," he encouraged as she freed him from the confines of denim and cotton. "Show me how much you want this."

His length sprang free, still impressive in its size and rigidity. Sam wrapped her fingers around him, marveling at the contrast between the silky skin and the steel hardness beneath. A bead of moisture had formed at the tip — clear, not at all blue. She couldn't help wondering at what point during his climax the color change occurred.

As if reading her mind, Ty threaded his fingers through her hair. "Why don't you find out for yourself?" he suggested, pulling her forward.

Sam's lips parted as she took him into her mouth. The musky, metallic taste of him flooded her senses, so different from Keith's milder flavor. She swirled her tongue experimentally around the head, gauging his reaction.

Ty's grip in her hair tightened suddenly, making her gasp. "Deeper," he commanded, his voice rough with desire. "Take more of me."

Without waiting for her to comply, he thrust forward, pushing himself deeper into her mouth. The unexpected motion made her eyes water, but instead of pulling back in protest as she might have done with Keith, Sam felt a thrill run through her. *This* was what she'd been missing for so long — this raw, unfiltered passion, this primal claiming.

"That's it," Ty groaned, setting a rhythm with his hips that had her struggling to accommodate him. "Use your tongue ... yes, like that."

His control was absolute, one hand fisted in her hair, the other gripping her jaw to angle her head exactly as he wanted. The domination sent waves of heat coursing through her body. Keith had always been so careful, so polite during their rare moments of oral intimacy, asking permission for the slightest change, apologizing if he thought he was being too demanding.

But this ... this was so different. Ty took what he wanted, used her mouth for his pleasure without apology. And God help her, she loved it.

"Look up at me," he ordered, tugging her hair sharply. "I want to see your eyes while you suck me."

Sam obeyed, raising her gaze to meet his. The intensity in those blue depths nearly undid her. His pupils were dilated with lust, leaving only a thin ring of color around the edges — and yet again, for the briefest instant, she thought she saw that vertical shape hinting through.

But then he thrust deeper, hitting the back of her throat, and all coherent thought fled. Sam relaxed her muscles, taking him further than she'd ever taken Keith, surrendering to his forceful pace.

"Such a good girl," Ty praised, his voice growing strained. "Taking all of me like you were *made* for it."

The praise sent a surge of pride through her, spurring her to greater efforts. She hollowed her cheeks, sucking harder, her hands coming up to grip his thighs for balance as he fucked her mouth with increasing urgency.

Tears streamed down her face from the intensity, but they weren't tears of distress — they were evidence of her complete surrender to the moment, to him. Each thrust pushed her further into a haze of arousal, her own need building despite the lack of direct stimulation.

"I'm getting close," Ty warned, his rhythm faltering slightly. "And you're going to swallow every drop, aren't you, Sam?"

She moaned her assent around his length, the vibration making him hiss with pleasure. His movements became erratic, his grip on her hair tightened to the point of pain as his body tensed.

Then, with a guttural groan, he erupted.

The first hot jet hit the back of Sam's throat, triggering her gag reflex. She struggled to swallow, but there was *so much* of it — far more than he had left inside her yesterday, far more than she'd ever known possible from any man. It just kept coming in powerful pulses, filling her mouth faster than she could manage.

Some escaped, trickling from one corner of her lips despite her best efforts to contain it all. The taste was overwhelming — like his smell, intensely musky with that strange metallic undertone that should have been repulsive but instead sent a thrill of forbidden pleasure through her core.

She moaned involuntarily, the vibration making Ty grunt above her.

"Swallow it," he commanded, his voice strained. "All of it."

Sam obeyed, gulping desperately, shocked to find herself savoring the unusual flavor. It sparked something primal within her, a craving she hadn't known existed until this moment. Her body responded with a rush of heat between her thighs, her arousal building to an almost painful intensity.

And when she thought he must surely be finished — when any normal man would have been far more than spent — Ty continued to pulse against her tongue, releasing yet another surge of his essence. Her eyes widened in disbelief, meeting his gaze. The blue of his irises seemed to glow with an internal light, watching her struggle to accommodate his seemingly endless release.

"That's it," he praised, his thumb caressing her stretched lips. "Take everything I have to give you."

Finally, at long last, the torrent subsided. Sam swallowed one last time, gasping for breath as Ty slowly withdrew from her mouth entirely. A thin strand of fluid — again faintly bluish, though not as obvious as yesterday — connected her lips to his still-hard member, breaking as he stepped back to admire her disheveled state.

"Beautiful," he murmured, his voice betraying sincere admiration. "And oh my! You still want more, don't you?"

Before she could respond, he hauled her to her feet and tore at her robe, exposing her trembling body to his hungry gaze.

"On your knees," he ordered, spinning her around to face the couch. "Hands on the cushions."

Sam wanted to ask for a moment to recuperate, but instead, she complied without hesitation, positioning herself as instructed. She felt exposed, vulnerable — and more aroused than she'd ever been in her life, even more than their first encounter. The cool air of the living room caressed her heated skin as she waited, breath shallow with anticipation.

Ty knelt behind her, his hands spreading her thighs wider. "So wet," he observed, one finger sliding through her folds. "All this from sucking me off? You really *are* made for this, aren't you, Sam?"

"Please," she whimpered, pushing back against his teasing touch. The cum in her belly felt as though it were percolating, making her hornier than ever. "I *need* you, I need you *inside* me!"

With a primal growl, Ty positioned himself at her entrance and thrust forward in one powerful motion. Sam cried out, a sharp gasp of mingled pleasure and pain as her tender tissues stretched to accommodate him again. Yesterday's vigorous coupling — added to Keith's less-vigorous intercourse — had left her sore, sensitive ... but instead of diminishing her pleasure, the edge of discomfort heightened every sensation, transforming the burning stretch into exquisite intensity.

"You're still tender from yesterday," Ty observed, his voice dropping to a silky purr as he slowed momentarily inside her. His fingers tightened on her hips, thumbs digging into the dimples at the base of her spine. "Does it hurt, Sam?"

"Yes," she admitted, her voice trembling. "But don't stop — *please* don't stop."

Ty leaned forward, his chest pressing against her back as his lips brushed her ear. "A little pain makes it better, doesn't it?" He withdrew almost completely before driving back in, deliberately rough. "That little ache reminds you who was here first. Who marked you as *his*."

Sam moaned, unable to deny the truth of his words. The lingering soreness made each thrust more intense, more present — a reminder of her previous transgression, and the forbidden nature of their current coupling.

"Answer me," he demanded, punctuating the command with a particularly deep thrust that made her gasp.

"Yes!" she cried, fingers clawing at the couch cushions. "God, yes — it hurts, but it's so good."

A dark chuckle rumbled through his chest. "I thought so." His pace increased, each powerful stroke sending shockwaves of sensation through her body. "Your husband couldn't make you feel this way if he tried. He's too ... gentle." The word dripped with contempt.

The mention of Keith should have doused her

arousal with guilt, but instead, it only intensified the forbidden thrill coursing through her veins. Sam pushed back against Ty's thrusts, meeting him halfway, surrendering to the delicious burn of overworked muscles and sensitive flesh.

"Look at you," Ty marveled, one hand sliding up her spine to fist in her hair, yanking her head back. "Taking me so well, even when you're hurting. Such a perfect little *vessel*."

The strange choice of words barely registered through the haze of sensation. Ty shifted his angle slightly, hitting a spot inside her that made stars burst behind her eyelids. The discomfort receded, overwhelmed by waves of building pleasure.

"I'm close," she gasped, feeling the telltale tightening in her lower belly. "Oh God, I'm so close—"

Without warning, Ty pulled out completely. Sam whimpered at the sudden emptiness, looking back over her shoulder in confusion.

"Not yet," he said, his voice containing an edge she hadn't heard before. "Turn around. I want to see your face when you come undone."

Sam obeyed, turning to face him, her legs trembling with need. Ty's expression was intense as he pushed her back onto the couch. He loomed over her, positioning himself between her spread thighs.

"That's better," he murmured, one hand caressing her flushed cheek. "I want to watch your eyes when it happens."

He entered her again in one fluid motion, filling her completely. Sam's back arched off the cushions, a keening moan escaping her lips. Ty established a relentless rhythm, each thrust deeper than the last, his gaze never leaving her face.

"Look at me," he commanded when her eyes threatened to flutter closed. "Don't you dare look away."

Sam forced her eyes open, locking onto his. She felt Ty began to stiffen and grow further inside her, and her own explosion swelled with him.

"Here we go," he hissed. "Take it all. Every drop. *Again.*"

As Ty's release flooded into her, Sam's entire body convulsed. The pleasure transcended anything physical she'd ever experienced, once again exceeding her previous round with Ty — a white-hot supernova exploding outward from her core, obliterating conscious thought. Her vision fractured into prismatic shards, sounds becoming distorted and distant as the room began to spin.

She struggled to stay awake this time, desperately fighting the encroaching darkness that threatened to swallow her. This sensation — this overwhelming, all-consuming ecstasy — she wanted so much to remain present for every single second of it, to burn it into her memory forever. But the intensity was too much for her mortal body to process ... and impossibly, it was still growing!

"I ... I can't ..." she gasped, her fingers clutching at his shoulders as yet another wave crashed through her, more powerful than the last. The edges of her vision darkened, tunneling inward as she battled to maintain consciousness.

"Feel it all," she heard Ty's voice, as though from far away. "Feel everything I'm giving you."

Sam's final awareness was of his eyes, so beautifully blue ... before the pleasure swelled once more, and the darkness claimed her completely.

7

When Samantha's consciousness surfaced again, she found herself floating in a strange, luminous space. Not darkness, not light, but something in between — a twilight realm of shifting blues and purples. She felt weightless, unbound by physical constraints, yet somehow more present in her body than ever before.

"Hello?" she called, her voice echoing. No answer came, but a warm sensation began to spread through her abdomen.

Sam looked down and gasped. Her previously flat stomach was now gently rounded, a small but unmistakable bump pushing against the fabric of a gossamer gown she didn't recognize. As she watched in wonder, the bump expanded, growing larger by the second.

"What's happening?" she whispered, but instead of fear, an inexplicable joy surged through her. Her hands moved to cradle her swelling belly, feeling it firm and warm beneath her palms.

The growth accelerated, her abdomen stretching outward as if months were passing in seconds. The sensation should have been painful, but instead felt blissful — an exquisite fullness that satisfied a hunger she hadn't fully acknowledged until this moment.

"This is what you've always wanted," came Ty's voice from everywhere and nowhere. "To be filled with

life."

True, so true. She and Keith spent the first years of their marriage trying to have children, to no avail, until the entire subject simply, quietly went away.

Now her belly continued its impossible expansion, so large she could no longer see her feet. The skin stretched taut and glowing, marked with delicate blue veins that pulsed with light. She felt movement inside — not one child, but many, shifting and turning in a synchronized dance.

"Three," she said with absolute certainty, though she couldn't explain how she knew. "There are three of them."

Her abdomen grew absurdly large, well beyond what should have been physically possible. She looked ten months pregnant with these three children, if such a thing could exist — her belly enormous, perfectly round, and straining against her skin. Yet there was no discomfort, only a profound sense of rightness and completion.

"My babies," she whispered, caressing the massive dome of her stomach with reverent hands. "Mine and Ty's."

The movement inside intensified, little limbs and bodies pushing against her from within. Sam laughed with pure delight, tears of joy streaming down her face.

"Perfect," she heard Ty say, his voice filled with satisfaction. "You were made for this, Samantha. Made to carry my offspring."

Those words should have disturbed her, should have triggered alarm bells ... but in this dream-state, they felt like the truest thing she'd ever heard: This was her purpose, her destiny. To be the vessel for these extraordinary lives growing within her.

"Yes," she agreed, her voice dreamy and distant. "I was made for this."

Her belly gave a final, dramatic expansion, stretching to a size that defied human anatomy. Sam embraced it, gloried in it, never wanting the feeling to end...

*   *   *

She woke with a gasp, her hand flying to her stomach — flat, unchanged. What had seemed so perfect, so desirable moments ago left her waking mind with a sense of unease.

But it was just a dream, a silly dream, no reason to get worked up over it. Or so she told herself.

Then she remembered where she was, and she bolted upright. The living room had darkened, shadows stretching across the floor as afternoon light filtered through the curtains. She was completely naked on the couch, the fabric cool and slightly damp beneath her bare skin.

"Ty?" she called, her voice hoarse. No answer came.

She fumbled for her phone on the coffee table. 2:47 PM. Once again, hours had passed since their encounter — hours she had passed in a faint, courtesy of that explosive climax. And once again, Ty had vanished without a word, leaving her unconscious and exposed.

"Damn it," she muttered, anger flaring through her post-coital haze. Twice now he'd reduced her to oblivion with pleasure unlike anything she'd ever experienced, and twice he'd slipped away without so much as a goodbye.

This time, the rudeness of it, the cavalier disregard, pierced through her lingering satisfaction.

She snatched her robe from the floor where Ty had tossed it and wrapped it tightly around herself, suddenly feeling vulnerable rather than sated. Keith would be home soon. She needed to shower, to erase the evidence of her afternoon transgression, especially Ty's—

That's when Sam realized something: She paused, waiting for the familiar sensation of fluid trickling down her thighs. But there was nothing. She pressed a hand between her legs, expecting to find the sticky evidence of their coupling.

Nothing.

Her breath hitched. She moved to the bathroom, examining herself in the mirror. Despite the intensity of their encounter, despite the copious amount she'd felt Ty release inside her — more than any normal man should be capable of producing, *especially* after how much she had previously swallowed while giving him head — there was no trace of it. Not a drop had leaked out.

"That doesn't make sense," she mumbled, her fingers probing gently. She was still slick with her own arousal, but Ty's semen — that strange, bluish fluid — had vanished completely. As if her body had absorbed it all.

She shook her head, determined not to make too much of this minor mystery. Because in spite of her irritation at his disappearing act, she could not deny she was already thinking about their next encounter.

She should feel ashamed ... but she didn't.

She turned on the shower, making the water as hot as she could stand it. As steam filled the bathroom, she rubbed over herself, especially around her mouth and between her thighs. She resisted the temptation to touch her vagina anywhere near her clitoris.

Under the spray, her thoughts returned to Ty's semen; not its absence, but its tremendous volume, and its blue tint, and his talk of a "rare condition" that now felt like a flimsy cover for something far more bizarre.

"Cyanosis," she murmured, remembering the term he'd used. But was that even real? Or had it been a convenient lie?

She shut off the water and grabbed a towel, drying herself with trembling hands. She needed to research this.

In the bedroom, Sam dressed quickly in jeans and a sweater, her damp hair leaving wet patches on the fabric. She retrieved her laptop and sat cross-legged on the bed, fingers flying over the keyboard.

"Cyanosis," she typed, her heart pounding.

As it turned out, Cyanosis *was* real, and it did have to do with decreased oxygen leaving a blue tint to subjects' bodies in various ways ... but nothing mentioned semen, nothing about Cyanosis affecting reproductive fluids.

She tried different combinations: "blue semen medical condition," and "unusual ejaculate volume" and "semen absorbed completely by body" Nothing that matched her experience.

So his form of Cyanosis was either *so* rare that it wasn't showing up in search engines ... or Ty was lying, for God only knew what reason.

And if he was lying about the color, he could be lying about his supposedly low sperm-count.

Jesus, she thought. *What if he gets me pregnant, for real?*

Yet again, the notion both terrified and aroused her. The thought of Ty taking her from behind, with her massive, baby-filled belly swaying beneath her ...

With a jolt, Sam realized she was rubbing herself through her jeans. She pulled her hand away through sheer force of will and straightened her posture, and the feeling of her sweater fabric dragging across her braless nipples aroused her further.

What the hell ...?

Sam was a sexual creature — as she was proving to a fault of late — but she had never been especially nipple-centric in her erogenous zones. Sure, she enjoyed it well enough when Keith played with them, but it was more the idea of the sexual interaction than the act itself that did it for her.

So what was *this* all about now?

Lifting her hands slowly, experimentally, to her breasts, she tweaked her nipples through her sweater. And it felt good, *really* good.

More curious than ever, she lowered her hands just long enough to reach up underneath her top.

Her fingertips found her nipples, which hardened further at her touch. A spike of pleasure, far more intense than she'd ever experienced from such simple stimulation, shot through her body. "Oh!" she gasped, shocked at her own sensitivity.

Tentatively, she rolled the hardened buds between her fingers, applying gentle pressure. The sensation was extraordinary — electric currents of pleasure radiating outward from her breasts, traveling down to pool between her thighs. Her breathing quickened as she continued the stimulation, pinching slightly harder. Each touch sent waves of delight cascading through her body, building with surprising speed. Her hips began to rock involuntarily against nothing but air, seeking friction that wasn't there.

She fell back against the pillows, both hands now working her nipples. The pleasure mounted impossibly fast, her internal muscles clenching rhythmically around emptiness. This shouldn't be possible, not for her — she'd never been able to climax from breast stimulation alone; not even close! — yet here she was, teetering on the precipice.

"Oh God," Sam moaned, arching her back as she twisted her nipples more firmly. The pressure built to an unbearable crescendo, and then — without any touch at all between her legs — she was cumming, her body convulsing in powerful waves of ecstasy. Stars burst behind her eyelids as she cried out, the orgasm rolling through her with shocking intensity.

When the spasms finally subsided, Sam lay motionless, dazed and trembling. That was ... unprecedented. She'd read about women who could orgasm from nipple stimulation alone, but she'd never, *ever* been one of them.

Until now, apparently.

"What's happening to me?" she asked the empty room.

As had so often been the case since first spying Ty soothing that feral cat, the mystery both scared her and turned her on beyond reason. Half of her wanted to stay the hell away from Ty, while the other half wished he were here, right now, shoving his cock into every hole on her body.

She repeated, "What is happening to me?"

And as before, the bedroom offered no answers.

8

The key turned in the lock at precisely 6:15 PM. Sam's heart skipped as she stirred the pasta sauce with more vigor than necessary, trying to appear casual.

"Something smells amazing!" Keith called, hanging his coat by the door.

Sam forced her lips into a smile. "Just spaghetti bolognese. Nothing special."

Keith approached from behind, wrapping his arms around her waist in a gentle hug. She almost flinched, then leaned back against him, compensating for her reaction.

"Long day?" he asked, his breath warm against her neck.

"Just the usual," she lied, turning to face him. His familiar features — the slight crook in his nose, the crow's feet forming at the corners of his eyes — suddenly seemed so ... safe. Boring, but *safe*.

Keith's brow furrowed as he studied her face. "You seem tense. Your trapezius is practically in your ears." His fingers brushed her shoulder. "Want me to work on that knot? Wouldn't take but a minute."

Sam shook her head. "No, thank you. I mean, I'm fine. Just, you know, focused on dinner." She forced a self-deprecating smirk. "Wouldn't want to mess up my spaghetti bolognese, now would I?"

Keith smiled back and nodded, but his eyes lingered on her face.

He helped set the table, filling the silence with stories from his practice — the elderly woman with the miraculous recovery, the teenager with the skateboarding injury. Sam nodded at appropriate intervals, her mind elsewhere.

After dinner, as they settled on the couch, Keith turned to her. "You know, I haven't given you a foot massage in ages. Remember how you used to beg for them when we first got married?"

The unexpected offer caught Sam off guard. It was true — she'd once loved his strong, methodical touch on her arches, the way his thumbs found every aching point. Before their sex life had faded into routine. Before the disappointment of negative pregnancy tests month after month.

"That would be ... nice," she said, surprising herself.

Keith patted his lap, and she swung her feet up. His hands were warm as they cradled her right foot, thumbs pressing into her arch with perfect pressure. Sam closed her eyes, guilt and pleasure mingling as she surrendered to his touch.

"You're carrying a lot of tension," Keith murmured, working his way up to her ankles. "Been painting a lot today?"

The question pierced her. Her easel had stood untouched all day. "Not really," she admitted.

He picked up on her disappointment. "That's okay. It'll keep coming back to you. Just you watch.

For now, just lay back and enjoy this."

Sam sank deeper into the couch cushions, surrendering to Keith's skilled touch. His thumbs pressed into the arch of her foot, releasing knots of tension she hadn't realized were there. A soft sigh escaped her lips as he worked his way methodically from her heel to her toes.

"That feels amazing," she murmured, her eyes fluttering closed.

As Keith's fingers moved to her ankle, then back to her instep, a curious warmth began to spread through her body. Each press of his thumbs sent tingles up her calves, her thighs ... reaching places that a simple foot massage had no business affecting. Her breathing quickened imperceptibly as the sensation intensified.

"Your skin's flushing," Keith observed, his voice holding a note of concern. "Am I pressing too hard?"

"No," Sam whispered, her voice strangely tight. "It's perfect. Don't stop."

The warmth transformed into something more insistent, more electric. Her hips shifted slightly against the couch as Keith's thumbs found a particularly sensitive spot beneath her arch. A jolt of pleasure shot straight to her core, making her gasp.

"Sam?" Keith's hands paused.

"Keep going," she urged, not quite recognizing her own voice.

He resumed, his movements slower now, more deliberate. Each press of his fingers sent waves of sensation cascading through her body. The pleasure built impossibly fast, coiling tight in her lower belly.

Sam bit her lip, trying to contain the mounting tension.

It was happening, *again* — that inexplicable hypersensitivity that had begun with her affair with Ty. Every nerve ending in her body seemed rewired, primed for pleasure at the slightest touch. She tried to fight it, to suppress the building orgasm, but Keith's innocent ministrations continued relentlessly.

When his thumb pressed firmly into the center of her arch, something inside her snapped. The tension broke in a sudden, sharp release that pulsed through her entire body. Sam clamped her jaw shut, stifling the moan that threatened to escape, her thighs clenching together as the small but unmistakable orgasm rippled through her.

But her efforts at discretion failed. A tiny, choked sound escaped her throat, and her body tensed visibly. Keith's hands slowed, then stilled.

"Did you just ...?" His voice trailed off, eyes widening as he studied her flushed face.

Sam couldn't speak, mortification washing over her in the aftermath of pleasure. She tried to pull her foot away, but Keith held it firmly.

"You did," he said, wonder replacing surprise in his tone. "From just this?"

She covered her face with her hands. "I'm sorry, I don't know— I didn't mean to—"

"Don't apologize," Keith interrupted, his voice dropping to a register she rarely heard from him. "That was ... incredibly hot."

Sam peeked through her fingers at him, took in the flush in his own cheeks.

"I want to make love to you," he whispered. "Right here, right now."

Sam froze, a new panic rising to replace her embarrassment. The thought of Keith inside her — where Ty had been just hours before — sent alarm bells ringing through her mind. What if some of Ty's strange blue-tinted semen remained? What if it somehow left a "stain" or whatever on Keith? Wouldn't he notice that? How could she explain it? The questions crashed through her like waves against a shore.

"Wait," she said, her voice steadier than she felt. She sat up, placing a hand on Keith's chest. "Let me ... let me pleasure you." Her lips curved into what she hoped was a seductive smile. "After all, it's your turn now."

Keith blinked, surprise evident on his face. "My turn?"

"Yeah," Sam continued, sliding from the couch to kneel between his legs. "You just gave me that *amazing* foot massage — you saw and heard how good it was, right? So ... it's *your* turn."

Her fingers worked at his belt buckle with practiced ease. Keith leaned back, a soft groan escaping his lips as she freed him from his trousers. He was already hard, his arousal evident.

"Sam, you don't have to—"

"I want to," she insisted, her voice husky. And she realized with a start that she *did* want this — wanted to bring him pleasure, to reconnect with her husband in some way that wouldn't betray her recent daytime activities. "Just relax and enjoy."

Keith surrendered, his head falling back against the couch cushions as Sam took him into her mouth.

The difference between Keith and Ty was immediately apparent. While Ty had stretched her lips and jaw to their limit, Keith's more modest size allowed her to take him completely without strain. A curious freedom overtook her as she realized she could experiment with techniques she'd never attempted with her husband before.

Sam relaxed her throat, allowed herself to slide down further, taking Keith deeper than she ever had. His sudden gasp of surprise and pleasure sent a thrill through her.

"Oh my God," Keith groaned, his fingers tentatively threading through her hair. "Sam, that's ... you've never ..."

She hummed in acknowledgment, the vibration making him twitch against her tongue. The ease with which she could control this experience was intoxicating. Where Ty had dominated her mouth with forceful thrusts, here she was the one in command, setting the pace, the depth, the pressure.

To her astonishment, as Keith's pleasure built, so did her own. Each moan from his lips seemed to resonate through her body, awakening echoes of arousal between her thighs. She hadn't touched herself, yet heat pooled in her core, building with each bob of her head.

"I'm getting close," Keith warned, his voice strained. "Sam, I'm going to—"

She didn't pull away as she sometimes did. Instead, she took him deeper, her nose brushing against his belly as his release hit the back of her throat. The taste was mild, so different from Ty's intense metallic flavor, and yet, as Keith's seed slid down her throat, something extraordinary happened: A sudden, unexpected orgasm ripped through her body, making her moan around his length. Her thighs trembled as waves of pleasure crashed through her, intense and unbidden, perfectly synchronized with Keith's climax.

When it subsided, Sam sat back on her heels, dazed and trembling. Keith stared at her, his expression a mixture of satisfaction and bewilderment.

"Did you just ...?" he asked for the second time that evening.

She nodded, unable to explain even to herself what had happened. Her body seemed to have developed a hair-trigger response to sexual stimulation of any kind — a response that had definitely not existed before Ty entered her life.

"That was incredible," Keith moaned, leaning down to kiss her forehead. "I don't know what's gotten into you lately, but I like it."

The irony of his choice of words wasn't lost on Sam. If he knew what — or who — had "gotten into her"...

Later that night, as Keith slept peacefully beside her, Sam stared at the ceiling, her mind racing. Something was happening to her body — something beyond normal arousal or desire. The inexplicable orgasms, the hypersensitivity, even her breasts' new responsiveness ... none of it made sense.

But she did know one thing: She liked it, and she wanted more, and more.

Sleep eventually claimed her, pulling her down into the depths of unconsciousness where her mind began to weave strange, vivid images ...

9

Samantha found herself in their bedroom, but it seemed larger somehow, more expansive, the walls fading into shadow at the edges of her awareness. The bed beneath her was impossibly soft, enveloping her naked body like a cloud. Moonlight streamed through gauzy curtains, casting everything in ethereal blue-white luminescence.

Keith appeared at the foot of the bed, his expression tender yet hungry in ways she rarely saw in waking life. He climbed onto the mattress, his body sleek and more defined than in reality, as if her dreaming mind had enhanced him.

"I've been waiting for you," she whispered, reaching for him.

His lips found hers, the kiss deep and consuming. His hands explored her body with newfound confidence, tracing paths of fire across her skin. Sam moaned into his mouth, arching against him.

"She's ready for us," came a voice from the shadows. Ty's voice.

Sam turned her head to see him materialize from the darkness, gloriously naked, his muscular form gleaming in the moonlight. His blue eyes glowed with an internal light that should have frightened her but instead sent waves of anticipation coursing through her body.

"*Both of you?*" *she asked, her voice husky with desire.*

Keith nodded, stroking her cheek. "We want to please you, Sam. Together."

Ty approached the other side of the bed, the mattress dipping under his weight. "Your body can take both of us. It was made to."

Her heart raced as they positioned themselves on either side of her, four hands now caressing her heated skin. Keith's touch was gentle, reverent, while Ty's was possessive, demanding. The contrast was intoxicating.

Keith lowered his head to her breast, taking a nipple between his lips. Simultaneously, Ty's mouth found her other breast, his tongue circling the sensitive peak before sucking hard. Sam gasped, her back arching off the bed at the dual sensation.

"More," she pleaded, her hands finding their heads, fingers tangling in their hair.

Ty's hand slid between her thighs, finding her already slick with arousal. His fingers parted her folds, circling her entrance teasingly. "So wet," he murmured against her breast. "So ready."

Keith's hand joined Ty's, his fingers finding her clit while Ty's probed deeper. The combined stimulation had her writhing between them, incoherent sounds of pleasure escaping her lips.

"I want to feel you inside me," she gasped to her husband.

Keith positioned himself between her thighs, his hardness pressing against her entrance. With one smooth thrust, he filled her, stretching her deliciously.

Then Ty rolled them over so that Sam was on top, and he positioned himself behind her, his hands gripping her hips to lift them slightly.

Understanding dawned on her face, a mixture of apprehension and excitement flickering across her features. She'd never experienced that particular act before, had always been too nervous to try it with Keith. And with both at the same time?!

"Relax," Ty murmured, his fingers trailing down the curve of her spine to the cleft of her buttocks. "Your body is ready for this. For both of us."

Ty's finger, slick with her own wetness, circled her puckered entrance, gently probing. Sam tensed initially, then forced herself to relax.

"That's it," he praised. "So perfect."

Then Ty finally positioned himself at her virgin entrance, and Sam held her breath. He pressed forward slowly ...

*   *   *

Sam's eyes snapped open.

The digital clock on the nightstand glowed 4:17 AM as Sam gasped for breath, her body slick with sweat and trembling with unfulfilled desire. Her hand flew between her legs, finding herself embarrassingly wet from the dream.

"Jesus ..." she whispered into the darkness.

Beside her, Keith slumbered peacefully, oblivious to her turmoil. Sam carefully extricated herself from the tangled sheets and padded to the bathroom, closing the door before turning on the light.

Her reflection startled her — flushed cheeks, dilated pupils, hair wild around her face. She splashed cold water on her skin, trying to calm her racing heart.

Relief washed over her as reality reasserted itself. It had just been a dream — vivid and exciting and unsettling, but a dream nonetheless. She hadn't actually participated in that taboo scenario with both men.

Yet alongside the relief came a gnawing frustration, an ache that lingered between her thighs. Part of her had wanted that dream to continue, wanted to experience the forbidden pleasure of being filled completely, possessed by both men at once.

"Okay," she told her reflection firmly, "this has to stop."

Ty was changing her into someone she barely recognized — someone who dreamed of sexual scenarios she'd never before considered, someone who could orgasm from a simple foot massage, someone who betrayed her husband without remorse.

As dawn broke, Samantha sat at the kitchen table nursing her third cup of coffee, a new resolve hardening within her. When Keith kissed her goodbye on his way to work, she returned it with genuine affection, guilt and determination mingling in her chest.

Once alone, she showered and dressed with particular care — jeans that hugged her curves, a soft sweater that accentuated her breasts without being overtly provocative. She applied minimal makeup, just enough to enhance her natural beauty.

Then she waited, knowing with inexplicable certainty that Ty would appear today.

By nine o'clock, the doorbell rang. Sam took a

deep breath, steadying herself before answering.

Ty stood on her threshold, looking as devastatingly handsome as ever in a simple black t-shirt and jeans. His blue eyes sparked with that now-familiar hunger as they swept over her.

"Morning, Sam," he purred, already stepping forward as if his entry was a foregone conclusion. And it was.

Sam had spent the past few hours determined to put her foot down. She had intended to demand to know a few things, first and foremost where the hell he got off disappearing on her each day after leaving her in a sex-addled stupor!

But as Ty entered her home yet again, as he reached for her breast with one hand and her hip with the other, her sexual desire exploded once more ...

... but it did not overcome her this time, not completely. She wanted, *needed* to have sex with Ty, right now, but her urge to take control of the situation also remained.

And this left her within a highly aroused, yet far less submissive mindset.

Sam planted her hands firmly on Ty's chest and pushed him backward. Surprise flickered across his attractive features as she continued advancing, forcing him to retreat until the backs of his legs hit the sofa.

"*My* turn," she said, her voice low and commanding. "Sit down."

Ty's eyebrows rose, but a slow smile spread across his face. "Assertive today, aren't we?"

"You have no idea," Sam replied, giving him one

final push that sent him sprawling onto the cushions.

She stood over him, legs slightly apart, hands on her hips. The power reversal sent a new thrill through her body — different from the surrendering pleasure she'd experienced before, but no less intoxicating. His eyes darkened as he looked up at her, that predatory hunger still evident, but now tinged with curiosity.

"Take off your shirt," she commanded.

Ty complied, pulling the black fabric over his head to reveal his sculpted torso. Sam's mouth watered at the sight, but she maintained her composure, determined not to lose herself to desire too quickly.

She straddled him, her knees on either side of his hips, careful to keep a few inches of space between their bodies. His hands immediately moved to her waist, but she caught his wrists, pinning them to the back of the couch.

"No touching," she whispered against his ear. "Not until I say so."

A flicker of something — frustration? amusement? — crossed his face. "And if I don't follow your rules?"

"Then I stop," Sam said simply, knowing it was the one threat that might work. "And we both know you don't want that."

Ty's jaw tightened, but he nodded once. "Your game, your rules. For now."

Sam smiled, feeling a surge of confidence. She released his wrists and began to undress, removing her sweater with deliberate slowness. Ty's eyes tracked every movement, his chest rising and falling with increasingly rapid breaths as she revealed her bare breasts.

"You're not wearing your bra today," he observed, his voice rougher than before.

"I didn't see the point," she replied, tracing her fingers down her own neck, between her breasts, watching his eyes follow the movement. "Not when I knew you'd be coming."

Her jeans followed, along with her panties, until she knelt naked above him, just out of reach. Ty's hands remained where she'd placed them, though his fingers curled into the fabric of the couch with visible restraint.

"Now you," she said, nodding at his remaining clothes.

Ty lifted his hips, allowing her to pull his jeans and underwear down his legs. His erection sprang free, impressively hard already. Sam licked her lips, remembering the taste of him, the impossible fullness when he filled her …

No! she scolded herself. *Stay in control.*

"You've been enjoying my body whenever you want," she said, stepping closer until her knees touched his. "Now I want something." She tangled her fingers in his dark hair, pulling his head forward. "Suck my nipples," she commanded, guiding his mouth to her breast.

Ty complied eagerly, his hot mouth closing around one sensitive peak. His tongue swirled expertly, sending electric currents of pleasure cascading through her body. Sam gasped, her head falling back as he alternated between gentle suction and teasing flicks.

"God, yes," she moaned, holding his head firmly against her chest. "Just like that."

The familiar tension began building rapidly, her body responding with that new, heightened sensitivity. Each pull of his mouth sent sparks straight to her core, the pressure mounting with shocking speed. She was already close, teetering on the edge of another nipple-induced climax.

But not yet. Not this time.

With tremendous effort, Sam pulled away, breaking the contact. Her nipple slipped from his mouth with an audible pop, glistening wet in the morning light. Ty looked up at her, confusion mingling with desire in his unnaturally blue eyes.

"I'm in charge today," she reminded him, her voice husky but firm.

Sam straddled his lap, positioning herself above his impressive length. She hovered there, teasing them both as she rubbed herself against the tip, coating him with her abundant wetness.

"Sam," Ty growled, his hands gripping her hips.

She captured his wrists, pushing them back against the sofa cushions. "No touching unless I say so, remember?"

With agonizing slowness, she lowered herself onto him, taking him inch by exquisite inch. Her body stretched to accommodate him, the delicious, now-familiar ache making her gasp. When he was fully seated within her, she paused, savoring the fullness.

"This is how it's going to be," she whispered, beginning to rock her hips in small, controlled movements. "My pace. My pleasure."

Ty's jaw clenched, his muscles taut with the effort of remaining still. "You're playing with fire," he warned, though his voice held a note of admiration.

"Maybe I like getting burned," Sam retorted, increasing her tempo gradually. She placed her hands on his shoulders for leverage as she began to rise and fall on his shaft, setting a rhythm that built her pleasure without rushing toward release.

The position allowed her complete control, letting her angle her body to hit exactly the spots she needed. Each downward stroke sent waves of sensation rippling through her.

Suddenly, Sam felt the familiar tightening in her core, the precipice of another mind-shattering orgasm approaching faster than she intended. No! She wasn't ready to surrender control, to be reduced to that quivering, unconscious state again. She *needed* to maintain her power in this encounter.

In a flash, the final moments of her dream returned to her — that forbidden act she'd never experienced in reality.

Without hesitation, she lifted herself until Ty slipped free from her body, earning a frustrated growl from him.

"What are you—?" he began, but his words died as Sam reached between her legs, gathering her abundant wetness on her fingers. With her eyes locked on his, she reached behind herself, using her slickness to prepare her untried entrance.

"I want you here," she whispered, positioning herself above him again, but differently this time. "I want to feel you everywhere."

Understanding dawned in Ty's eyes, and while she expected him to enjoy the idea of this, she noticed something beneath his arousal. Was that ... dissatisfaction?

"Fine," he said in a flat tone. "You're in control today."

And since she *was* in control, Sam chose to ignore his dulled enthusiasm and enjoy this herself.

The pressure was intense, bordering on pain as the head of his cock breached her virgin entrance. Sam gasped, freezing in place as her body adjusted to the unfamiliar intrusion. Then she focused on her breathing as she eased down another fraction of an inch. The burning stretch gradually transformed into something else — a fullness that sent new, unexplored sensations radiating through her body.

Inch by excruciating inch, Sam lowered herself until she had taken almost all of him, her thighs trembling with the effort. The sensation was overwhelming — different from vaginal penetration, more intense, more taboo. She felt utterly possessed, completely filled in a way she'd never imagined possible. But there was some pain, too.

"Move," she commanded, though her voice shook slightly.

Ty shifted his hands to her hips, guiding her movements as he began thrusting upward with careful control. The sensations of his cock sliding inside her forbidden passage had Sam gasping, her head falling back in surrender.

The fusion of pleasure and pain built rapidly

within her as Ty thrust over and over. Sam's body quivered on the edge of climax, her inner muscles clenching around his invasion. The burning discomfort kept her tethered to reality even as waves of pleasure threatened to pull her under.

"Oh God," she gasped, her fingernails digging into his shoulders. "I'm going to—"

The orgasm crashed through her like lightning striking earth, electric and violent. Her vision blurred at the edges ... but this time, it didn't fade completely to black as it had before. The pain counterbalanced the pleasure, keeping her consciousness intact, though barely. Her body convulsed around him, the contractions wringing out every last sensation.

Ty stilled beneath her, his face contorted not in pleasure but in frustration. With not much gentleness, he lifted her trembling body off him and laid her on the couch. Then he stood and began dressing himself.

Sam lay still, "playing possum" for lack of a better phrase.

Then Ty grumbled *something* under his breath. She didn't understand any of it — in fact, she was fairly certain that it wasn't even English.

Once fully dressed, he strode to the door and left, slamming it behind him.

She stood up from the couch, steadied herself, then hurried to the front window.

West, she thought to herself. *He's walking west.*

Why did that matter? She supposed it really didn't.

So why had she made note of it?

Because he's never told me where he lives, she

realized. *Just some vague comment about "the house at the end of the block."*

That's right. But which house? And how far down did he consider "the end of the block"?

Part of her felt silly. She had taken the man in her mouth, pussy, and now even her ass, and *now* she's worried about where he lives?

Shaking her head at herself, she headed for yet another shower.

10

Later that morning, Sam experienced changes in herself she simply could not brush off or ignore. The first was disturbing, but also the least surprising, given how her body had been behaving.

Freshly showered once more, she sat on the edge of her bed, a strange emptiness gnawing at her despite the anal encounter with Ty. The relatively milder orgasm, and his abrupt departure, had left her feeling hollow, unsatisfied in a way that transcended the physical. Her body thrummed with residual arousal, an insistent pulse between her thighs that wouldn't subside.

"Damn it," she whispered, falling back against the mattress.

Before she could second-guess herself, her hand slid beneath the towel wrapped around her body. Her fingers found her still-sensitive folds, slick with renewed arousal. The first touch sent a jolt through her system so intense she gasped aloud. Her body responded with unprecedented eagerness, as if starved for stimulation despite the multiple orgasms she'd experienced over the past days.

She circled her clit once, twice ... and on just the third pass, her body detonated. The orgasm slammed into her with the force of a freight train, her back arching off the bed as pleasure radiated outward from her core in violent waves. Her mouth opened in a silent scream, the intensity robbing her of voice, of breath, of thought.

"Oh ... my ... God!" she choked out when she could finally speak, her hand falling away from her center.

Except the orgasm didn't stop.

Sam's eyes flew open in shock as the contractions continued to pulse through her, gaining momentum rather than subsiding. Her thighs trembled uncontrollably, muscles spasming without her command. The pleasure built impossibly higher, cresting again and again in an endless surge that had her writhing against the sheets.

"What's happening?" she gasped, clutching at the bedspread as another wave crashed through her. Her untouched nipples had hardened to almost painful points, her skin hypersensitive to even the air currents in the room.

Two minutes passed. Then three. The relentless ecstasy showed no signs of abating. Sam's consciousness began to fragment, reality dissolving around the edges as her nervous system overloaded with stimulation. Sweat drenched her body, her lungs burning as she struggled to draw breath between spasms.

"Please," she panted, though she wasn't sure if she was begging for it to stop or continue forever. "Please, please, please ..."

By the fifth minute, Sam's vision had tunneled to pinpoints of light. Her heart hammered dangerously fast in her chest, her limbs jerking involuntarily as the pleasure turned arduous in its intensity.

Just as darkness began to close in around her, the contractions finally began to slow, her body giving one last shuddering pulse before gradually going limp.

Sam lay motionless on the bed, utterly spent, hovering on the edge of consciousness. Her mind struggled to process what had just happened: an orgasm that continued long after stimulation ceased, that nearly rendered her unconscious with its ferocity.

This isn't normal, she thought. Then she repeated aloud, "This isn't *normal*."

She noticed the next changes when she finally had the energy to get dressed: Her bra was loose. No, not the bra itself, not overall — the *cups* of her bra were loose.

Frowning, Sam pulled the bra straps tighter, but the cups still gaped around her chest. Had the garment stretched in the wash? She tossed it aside and reached for another, one of her favorites that always fit perfectly.

Same result.

She stood before the full-length mirror, naked and perplexed. Her breasts looked ... different, a little smaller. Sam cupped them in her palms, feeling their weight. Where they had once filled her hands completely, now there was some space left over, but as she hefted them, they *seemed* to feel about the same weight as ever.

"What the hell?" she whispered, turning sideways to examine her profile.

The reduction was unmistakable. Her

once-generous C-cups (sometimes D in certain brands) had shrunk to what looked like full B-cups.

But the size wasn't the only change. The skin felt different under her fingertips — tighter, firmer, more youthful, like when they first started growing in her early teens.

Her nipples, too, had transformed. They seemed longer, more prominent even in their relaxed state. Sam ran a tentative finger over one and gasped at the immediate, electric response. Still that incredible sensitivity, perhaps even more intense now.

Then she leaned closer to the mirror, squinting at her reflection, and her blood turned to ice water in her veins.

"No," she breathed, touching her areola with trembling fingers. "That's not possible."

Around each nipple, the normally pink flesh had taken on a subtle bluish tint — the same cerulean shade as Ty's semen. The discoloration was faint enough that someone else might not notice immediately, but to Sam's horrified gaze, it stood out like a beacon.

"Oh God," she whispered, backing away from the mirror. "What's happening to me?"

Her mind raced through possibilities, each more terrifying than the last. Was it some kind of infection? A bizarre allergic reaction to Ty's semen?

Sam fumbled for her phone, her first instinct to call a doctor. But what would she say? "Hello, my breasts have shrunk overnight and turned blue after I had sex with a man who ejaculates blue-tinted semen"?

Even if she weren't concerned they might commit her for psychiatric evaluation, this would expose her extramarital activities — Keith would learn she'd been cheating on him.

Stressing about what to do, Samantha began pacing back and forth across her bedroom ... which is when she noticed yet another change.

As Sam stepped back and forth on the carpeted floor, a strange sensation along the soles of her feet made her pause. With each step, the plush carpet fibers seemed to tickle and stimulate her feet in ways she'd never experienced before.

"What now?" she muttered, sitting back on the bed to examine the bottoms of her feet. And what she found confused her more than the changes in her breasts.

The usual rough patches — the natural calluses built up from decades of walking — had completely disappeared. She ran her fingertips along her heels, the balls of her feet, under her toes, finding nothing but impossibly smooth, pink skin. Her feet looked brand new, like a baby's, unmarked by life or use.

"That's ... impossible," she whispered, something she'd found herself saying a lot recently.

She pressed harder on her soles, searching for the familiar tough spots that should have been there. When she touched a particularly sensitive area in the center of her arch, a jolt of pleasure shot up her leg and into her core, making her gasp — and reminding her of her orgasming from Keith's simple foot massage.

Sam carefully stood, wincing slightly at the

tenderness. Without the protective layer of calluses, every sensation was amplified — the texture of the carpet, the cool hardwood in the hallway, the slick tile of the bathroom floor. Each surface sent different signals racing up her nervous system, some merely intense, others distinctly pleasurable.

She gripped the bathroom counter, staring at her reflection. Her pupils were dilated, her cheeks flushed just from walking across the house. The woman in the mirror looked feverish.

"What's happening to me?" she asked her reflection for what felt like the hundredth time.

Samantha pulled on a pair of thick, fuzzy socks she normally saved for winter, hoping they might cushion her newly sensitive feet. Even the gentle pressure of cotton against her skin sent ripples of sensation up her legs. She dressed quickly in loose clothing that wouldn't rub against her altered breasts, avoiding looking at her reflection again.

Maybe painting would help. Art had always been her refuge, her way of processing emotions too complex for words. She set up her easel by the window where natural light streamed in, arranging her paints and brushes with methodical care.

The moment her fingers closed around her favorite sable brush, something felt wrong. The wooden handle that should have fit perfectly into the grooves worn into her skin over years of use now felt alien against her grip. Sam frowned, adjusting her hold, but the familiar connection between hand and tool remained elusive.

She turned her hand palm-up, examining her

fingers closely. The hardened patches of skin along the side of her middle finger, the ridge of her palm where the brush typically rested — they were gone. Her painter's hand had transformed overnight into something impossibly smooth and unblemished, as if she'd never held a brush in her life.

First she turned into an orgasm machine, then her breasts changed, then her feet, now her painting hand?!

Sam dipped the brush into cobalt blue paint with trembling fingers. The color reminded her of Ty's eyes, of the strange fluid he'd left inside her, of the subtle tint now coloring her areolas. She pressed the brush to canvas, trying to lose herself in the familiar motion, but everything felt wrong — the pressure, the angle, the way the bristles dragged across the surface.

Without the calluses that had developed over years of practice, she no longer controlled the brush with her adept precision. Frustration welled up as she tried to capture the image in her mind, but her hand wouldn't cooperate.

"Damn it!" She flung the brush across the room, where it left a streak of blue against the wall before clattering to the floor.

As funny as it might sound to an outsider — or perhaps to any non-artist — this was the moment she felt that she broke free from Ty's "spell" over her. Not her out-of-control sex drive, not the inexplicable alterations to her body … but the simple, negative impact it was having on her artwork.

Would she have been up for sex at that very moment? Hell yeah. But was she at all interested in having *Ty* as her partner?

No. No, she didn't think so. If his naked, throbbing cock were in front of her face she might feel differently ... but in his absence, she no longer yearned for his return.

11

Shortly after she ate lunch, the thought hit Sam with such force that she had to sit down:

Pregnant.

The word reverberated through her mind like a thunderclap. What if all these changes — her hypersensitivity, her transforming body, the bluish tint to her areolas — weren't some strange infection or allergic reaction? What if they were symptoms of something far more profound?

"Oh my God," she whispered, her hand instinctively moving to her still-flat abdomen. *What if I'm pregnant with Ty's baby?*

She remembered his words about his "rare condition" causing a low sperm count. But what if the opposite was true? What if his blue-tinted ejaculate was exceptionally potent?

Her mind raced through the changes her body had undergone. The heightened sensitivity, the physical alterations — none of it matched normal pregnancy symptoms, especially not mere *days* after conception.

But then, who knew what blue-tinted semen could do?

A pregnancy test — that was the logical next step. Even if this was something outside a normal pregnancy, the test might still detect hormonal changes. It would be better than wild speculation and mounting panic.

Grabbing her purse from the counter, she headed toward the front door with determined strides. But as she bent to retrieve her sneakers from the shoe rack, her loose-fitting shirt dragged across her transformed nipples. The sensation was electric, sending a jolt of pleasure so intense that she nearly collapsed.

"Jesus," she gasped, steadying herself against the wall.

She succeeded on getting her shoes on her next attempt, but then her thick socks had to come off. The soles of her newly delicate feet slipping into regular socks and then the shoes created a symphony of sensation that traveled up her legs and pooled between her thighs. The dual stimulation — her longer nipples, followed by her softened feet — triggered an immediate, overwhelming arousal that left her trembling.

Damn it, there was no way she could go out like this. Not when the slightest friction against her altered body threatened to reduce her to a quivering, moaning mess in public. She needed release first, needed to take the edge off this maddening sensitivity.

Sam stumbled back to the living room couch, already pulling her shirt over her head. Her hands flew to her smaller, firmer breasts, cupping them gently. Even that light touch was almost too much to bear. Her head fell back against the cushions as she began to circle her slightly-bluish nipples with trembling fingers.

"Mmmm ..." she whimpered as pleasure spiraled

through her with frightening speed.

She barely had time to slip her other hand beneath the waistband of her pants before the orgasm hit her — another explosion of sensation that arched her back and tore a cry from her throat. Her body convulsed, muscles contracting rhythmically as wave after wave of ecstasy crashed through her.

Thankfully, unlike before, this climax did not extend endlessly. It peaked sharply, intensely, then ebbed away, leaving her gasping but coherent. Her mind cleared almost immediately, the edge of desperate need dulled enough that she could function.

"Okay," she panted, pushing herself upright. "Now I can go."

The drive to the pharmacy was a study in concentration. Every bump in the road, every vibration of the car seat, sent ripples of pleasure through her hypersensitive body. Sam gripped the steering wheel with white knuckles, focusing on her breathing to maintain control.

When she finally pulled into the pharmacy parking lot, she sat motionless for several minutes, gathering herself.

In and out, she told herself. *That's it. Then you can go home, and find out.*

Inside the brightly lit drugstore, Sam made her way directly to the family planning aisle. The rows of pregnancy tests overwhelmed her — digital, early detection, strips, plus signs. She grabbed the most expensive one, figuring it might be the most accurate, and turned to head to the checkout.

"Sam? Is that you?"

She froze at the familiar voice. Jessica Martinez, her neighbor and friend since college, stood at the end of the aisle, her curly brown hair pulled into a messy bun, wearing torn jeans and an oversized sweater — her typical work-from-home attire.

"Jessie," Sam managed, instinctively trying to hide the pregnancy test behind her back. "What are you doing here?"

Jessica held up a bottle of allergy medication. "Pollen season is killing me." Her hazel eyes darted to Sam's poorly concealed purchase, then widened with excitement. "Oh my God! Are you—?" She lowered her voice to a dramatic whisper. "Are you and Keith *finally* expecting?"

Heat flooded Sam's face. "I ... I'm not sure yet. It's just to check."

"That's amazing!" Jessica squealed, bouncing on her toes. "I know how long you two have been trying. Keith must be over the moon just at the possibility!"

The mention of Keith sent a wave of guilt crashing through Sam. "No, I'm ... I'm keeping it to myself, for now. You know, just in case it's another false alarm."

"Of course, of course." Jessica pantomimed zipping her lips, though her eyes still sparkled with excitement. "But if it's positive, we're definitely celebrating. I'll bring that sparkling cider you like — the fancy French one."

Sam nodded weakly, desperately wanting to escape this conversation. Her body was again humming with unresolved arousal, and the fear of carrying Ty's child made her light-headed.

"You okay?" Jessica frowned, stepping closer. "You look a little flushed."

"Fine," Sam said quickly. "Just nervous about the test."

Jessica squeezed her arm sympathetically. "Well, whatever happens, I'm here for you. And Sam?" Her expression grew uncharacteristically serious. "You're going to be an amazing mom. I've always thought so."

The sincerity in her friend's voice made Sam's throat tighten. If Jessica only knew the truth — that this potential pregnancy wasn't Keith's at all, but the result of a bizarre affair with a complete and total stranger who just happened ...

... who just happened to have moved into their neighborhood.

But had he?

Sam realized with a start that she'd never actually verified Ty's story about inheriting a house nearby — from his uncle, was it?

"Hey, Jess," Sam said, the words tumbling out before she could reconsider, "you know everyone around here. Have you met our new neighbor? Guy named Ty Boxx — with two Xs, he made a point of telling me."

Jessica's brow furrowed, her head tilting slightly. "New neighbor? Where exactly?"

"He said he inherited a house at the end of the block — from his uncle, I think," Sam explained, watching her friend's face carefully.

Jessica shook her head slowly. "Sam, there's no new neighbor anywhere near us. I'm friends with

Melanie from Cornerstone Realty, remember? She handles most of the properties in our area. I was just having drinks with her last weekend, and she mentioned how dead the market's been — nothing's sold *or* changed hands in our neighborhood for at least eight months."

Sam felt the blood drain from her face. "That's ... are you sure?"

"I'm positive," Jessica insisted. "Mel would have mentioned it — she complains about her commission drought constantly. If someone inherited a place, she'd've known about that, too." She studied Sam's expression with growing concern. "Why? Who is this guy claiming to live near you?"

"I ..." Sam's mind raced, searching for a plausible explanation. "Just someone I've seen around a few times. He, uh, seems to have an affinity for stray cats. Said he moved in recently."

Jessica's eyes narrowed slightly. "What does he look like?"

"Tall, dark hair, really blue eyes," Sam answered automatically, then wished she hadn't been so specific.

"Hmm," Jessica tapped her lip thoughtfully. "Doesn't ring any bells. Maybe he's renting? Or staying with someone while he *hopes* to inherit?"

"Maybe," Sam agreed weakly, her heart pounding so loudly she was certain Jessica must hear it.

"Want me to ask Mel to check?" Jessica offered. "She could tell us if anyone named 'Boxx' owns property anywhere nearby."

"No, but thanks," Sam replied, perhaps a little

too quickly. "I mean, it's not important. Just making conversation."

Jessica gave her an odd look but didn't press further. "Okay ... well, I should get going. Let me know about the test, yeah? Fingers crossed!"

Sam nodded, forcing a smile as Jessica squeezed her arm once more before heading to the checkout.

Once alone, Sam leaned heavily against the shelf, her mind reeling. Ty had lied about inheriting some house. And possibly about his so-called medical condition. What else had he lied about? His intentions?

Who the hell *was* Ty Boxx?

As she turned around to head toward checkout, her top and pants and shoes all rubbed just the right way — or the *wrong* way — to re-spark her arousal.

Damn it, this is turning from exciting into an affliction.

On pure impulse, she changed aisles and, making sure Jessica was nowhere in sight, Sam picked up a "discreetly packaged" vibrator, the smallest one they seemed to carry.

Then she headed back for checkout, and home.

<h1 style="text-align:center">12</h1>

Sam's hands trembled as she clutched the small plastic stick, watching the indicator window with dread. One line. Just one line appeared, growing steadily more distinct against the white background. She released a breath she hadn't realized she'd been holding, her shoulders sagging as tension drained from her body.

"Not pregnant," she whispered to the empty bathroom.

Relief washed over her. For a few years there, she and Keith had been trying, charting cycles, timing intercourse, even standing on her head afterward once when a friend swore it had worked for her. Yet now, after her encounter with Ty, the negative result felt like salvation.

She wrapped the test in toilet paper and buried it deep in the bathroom trash, not wanting Keith to see it. He'd ask questions — when had she taken it, why hadn't she waited for him to be home. Questions she didn't have innocent answers for.

Sam splashed cold water on her face, studying her reflection. The woman in the mirror looked the same, but something had shifted inside her. The bathroom light caught the gold of her wedding band as she gripped the edge of the sink.

"What are you doing, Samantha?" she asked her reflection. "What *have* you been doing?"

Then — once again — her libido reared its insatiable head.

Sam rolled her eyes. "Fine," she told her body aloud. "But this time I've prepared for you."

Returning to the pharmacy bag she'd casually dropped onto the bed, Sam pulled out her new vibrator. It really was kind of small, but this round was going to be less about pleasure, more about maintenance and control.

Popping in the complimentary, generic battery, she turned the device on. It only came with one setting, but seemed powerful enough.

Getting rid of her pants and underwear, Sam climbed onto the bed.

She positioned the vibrator against her clitoris, gasping at the instant jolt of pleasure that shot through her body. Even with such a small vibrator, the sensation was almost too intense with her new hypersensitivity. Sam bit her lip, determined to maintain control this time — a quick release to take the edge off, then back to figuring out what was happening to her.

"Just a quickie," she stated aloud, closing her eyes as she circled the vibrating tip around her sensitive bud.

The response was immediate and overwhelming. Her back arched off the bed as pleasure radiated outward from her core, building with frightening speed. Her thighs began to tremble, muscles tensing as she hurtled toward climax after less than thirty seconds of stimulation.

"Oh God," she gasped, the orgasm washing over her in powerful waves. Her hips bucked involuntarily, causing the vibrator to slide lower ...

As the initial peak began to subside, the tip of the device slipped between her folds, and with a sudden internal contraction, was sucked completely inside her.

Sam's eyes flew open in shock. "No!" she cried, the word transforming into a strangled moan as the vibrator continued buzzing deep within her. The sensation was unlike anything she'd experienced — more invasive and all-consuming than anything Ty or Keith had ever made her feel.

She reached down frantically, trying to retrieve the device, but with her intense trembling, her fingers couldn't gain purchase. Each attempt to grasp it pushed it deeper, pressing it against spots inside her that sent lightning bolts of pleasure cascading through her nervous system.

"Oh no, no, no ..." she panted, her body betraying her as another orgasm built with terrifying intensity. Her internal muscles clenched around the intruder, holding it in place as it continued its relentless vibration against her most sensitive inner walls.

The second climax hit harder than the first, wrenching a scream from her throat that she barely muffled with a pillow. Stars burst behind her eyelids as her consciousness threatened to slip away, but the constant, unrelenting stimulation kept her tethered to awareness — there would be no escape into unconsciousness this time.

When the peak finally ebbed, Sam lay gasping, sweat dampening her skin. She tried again to remove the vibrator, pushing her fingers inside herself, but the attempt only triggered another series of contractions that drove the device against her G-spot, sending her spiraling into a third orgasm.

"Please," she sobbed — though, as with her touch-less 5-minute orgasm, she wasn't sure if she was begging for it to stop or continue. Her body had become a conduit for endless waves of pleasure, each one cresting before the previous had fully receded.

Minutes stretched into a quarter hour, then half an hour. Sam lost count of her orgasms — they blurred together into one continuous surge of sensation that left her trembling, soaked in sweat, throat raw from suppressed screams. The sheets beneath her were drenched, her limbs weak from constant tension as her muscles contracted over and over. The vibrator's buzz seemed to intensify rather than diminish, its relentless mechanical rhythm never slowing, never tiring as a human partner would.

Time lost all meaning as Sam had no choice but to surrender to the inescapable pleasure. Her world narrowed to the pulsing heat between her thighs, the constant stimulation that drove her to heights she'd never imagined possible. Tears streamed down her face, mingling with the sweat that plastered her hair to her forehead.

"Make it stop ..." she whimpered, her voice barely audible, yet even as she begged for relief, her hips rocked against the mattress, chasing the next peak. Her body had become a stranger to her, operating on primal instincts beyond her control.

By the time the first hour passed, Sam had entered an altered state of consciousness. The constant orgasms had pushed her into a liminal space where pleasure and frustration blurred together, where her mind floated somewhere above her convulsing body. Her fingernails clawed at the sheets, her teeth bit at her pillow case.

"I can't ... take much more ..." she breathed.

But the vibrator continued its merciless assault, buzzing away inside her, triggering wave after wave of spasms. Her thighs had stopped trembling, not from relief but from sheer exhaustion — the muscles simply had nothing left to give. Still, her internal walls contracted rhythmically, milking sensation from the unyielding device.

Entering the second hour brought delirium. Sam's consciousness fractured into pieces, some floating far above, watching her writhing form with detached curiosity, others sinking deep into the center of each orgasm, exploring the endless variations of pleasure that coursed through her oversensitized nervous system.

Colors swirled behind her closed eyelids — electric blues reminiscent of Ty's eyes, his strange semen. Visions flickered through her mind: her body swollen with impossible pregnancies, her skin taking on that same cerulean tint, Ty watching her with predatory satisfaction.

Just when Sam thought she would lose her mind completely, the vibrator's buzz began to falter. The mechanical hum stuttered, its rhythm becoming erratic. Hope sparked through her delirium as the device's power finally, mercifully began to fade.

"Thank ... God ..." she choked, her voice a broken rasp.

The vibrations weakened further, pulsing with decreasing strength until, with one final pathetic buzz, the battery died completely.

The sudden silence was deafening. Sam lay motionless, her body still twitching with aftershocks, unable to summon the strength to move. Her consciousness slowly knitted itself back together after that endless stimulation ceased, reality reasserting itself in painful increments.

Minutes passed before she could even lift a hand to wipe the sweat from her face.

The vibrator, now silent and still, remained lodged inside her. With trembling fingers, Sam finally managed to extract it, wincing as it slid free from her swollen, hypersensitive flesh. She stared at the innocuous-looking device, marveling that something so small had reduced her to such a state.

"That was ..." she whispered, unable to find words adequate to describe what she'd just experienced. No human being should be capable of enduring such prolonged, intense pleasure without losing consciousness or suffering some physical damage — if *nothing* else, the vibrations should have caused her vagina to go *numb* at some point. Yet it hadn't, and here she was, spent but still intact.

A strange clarity settled over her as her breathing gradually returned to normal. The fog of obsession that had surrounded thoughts of Ty since their first encounter seemed to have lifted, burned away by the excessive stimulation she'd just endured. His magnificent body, those piercing blue eyes, even his impressive manhood — they no longer held the same hypnotic power over her imagination.

"Been there, done that ... and then some," she murmured with a weak laugh. Whatever primal spell he'd cast over her had been broken by the mechanical substitute that had just driven her beyond any pleasure he could provide.

And yet ... funny enough — or perhaps *appropriate* enough — the notion of making love to Keith again did hold some appeal. Not right now, of course! But the idea of having her husband moving inside her ... that was a lingering spark that she could see returning to a flame.

Keith ... not Ty. *Keith.*

Sam rolled to her side, gathering her strength before pushing herself up on shaky arms. Her legs felt like jelly, refusing to support her weight initially. She crawled across the bed, pausing at the edge to catch her breath before attempting to stand.

The bathroom seemed miles away as she staggered forward, using the wall for support. Each step was a monumental effort, her muscles protesting after hours of continuous tension. The cool tile beneath her feet sent another shiver of sensation up her legs, but it was muted now, bearable.

She reached the shower and turned the knob,

leaning heavily against the glass door as steam began to fill the small space. The sound of running water drowned out her ragged breathing, offering a comforting white noise after the mechanical buzz that had dominated her senses.

13

The doorbell rang just as Sam was slipping into a loose cotton dress, her skin still dewy from the shower. She froze, heart pounding. Who could that be? Please, not Ty again ...

She padded to the front door on her sensitive bare feet, peering through the peephole. Relief washed through her when she saw Keith standing there, laden with grocery bags. He was home early again.

"Hey!" he called as she opened the door. "Thought I'd surprise you. Got stuff for a proper dinner tonight."

Sam smiled, genuinely happy to see him. "You're a sight for sore eyes."

Keith paused as he set the bags on the counter, studying her face. "You seem ... different." His head tilted slightly. "*Good* different. Relaxed."

"Do I?" She tucked a strand of damp hair behind her ear.

"Yeah." He approached slowly, as if drawn by some invisible force. "There's something about you today."

His fingers brushed her cheek with a tenderness that made her throat tighten. Without the frantic arousal that had consumed her lately, Sam could appreciate the simple warmth of his touch, the familiar scent of his aftershave.

"I've been thinking about you all day," Keith admitted, his voice dropping lower as he drew her against him. "Couldn't focus on my patients."

His lips found hers, gentle at first, then with growing hunger. Sam melted into the kiss, her arms winding around his neck. After the untamed trysts with Ty and the mechanical frenzy of the vibrator, this human connection felt like coming home.

"The groceries can wait," Keith murmured against her neck, hands sliding down to her hips.

Sam nodded, allowing him to lead her up to their bedroom. His eagerness was flattering, especially after months of dwindling passion between them. But where before she might have matched his urgency, now she felt a different kind of desire — slower, deeper, more connected.

As they reached the bed — which she had thankfully changed after its sweat-soaked state — Keith's hands moved to the hem of her dress, but Sam gently caught his wrists. "Slow," she whispered. "Let's take our time."

Something in her tone made him pause. His eyes searched hers, finding not rejection but invitation to something more meaningful.

"I just want to feel you," she explained, guiding him to sit on the edge of the bed. She stood between his knees, cradling his face in her palms. "Really *feel* you."

Keith nodded, his breath catching as she leaned down to kiss him with deliberate slowness. Their lips moved together in a familiar dance, yet somehow new, as if they were rediscovering each other.

Sam unbuttoned his shirt with unhurried movements, pausing to touch each newly revealed inch of skin. Where Ty had been all frantic passion and possession, this was exploration and appreciation. She traced the curve of Keith's collarbone, the slight softness around his middle that spoke of comfortable years together.

"You're beautiful," she whispered, the words holding a weight they hadn't carried for some time. She meant it — truly, genuinely meant it.

Keith's eyes softened at her words, his hands settling on her waist with a gentle pressure that spoke of desire tempered by devotion. When he pulled her down to the mattress beside him, Sam went willingly, her body curving into his with practiced ease.

Their clothes fell away gradually, each garment removed with reverence rather than rushed necessity. Sam guided Keith's hands to her transformed breasts, watching his face carefully for any sign he noticed the changes. But his expression showed only appreciation and desire as he caressed her with familiar tenderness.

"I want to feel all of you," she murmured, drawing him above her.

As Keith entered her, Sam sighed, not with the explosive pleasure that had marked her encounters with Ty, but with a deep, soul-level contentment. She moved beneath him unhurriedly, focusing on the connection between them rather than chasing the peak she knew her altered body could reach in seconds.

"God, Sam," Keith breathed against her neck, his

movements steady and measured. "You feel incredible."

She wrapped her legs loosely around his waist, hands tracing patterns on his back as they rocked together. The physical sensations were present — her body still responded with that new heightened sensitivity — but she deliberately kept herself anchored in the emotional experience, in the intimacy of being with the man she had built a life alongside.

"I love you," she whispered, and found herself blinking back unexpected tears.

Keith kissed her deeply in response, his rhythm faltering slightly at her words. His breathing quickened, muscles tensing beneath her fingertips as he approached his climax.

"Sam, I'm—" he gasped, his movements becoming more urgent.

"It's okay," she assured him, holding him close as he shuddered against her, his release washing through him in gentle waves rather than the violent torrent that had marked Ty's completion.

As Keith collapsed against her, his breath warm against her shoulder, Sam felt a lingering ache of unfulfilled need. Not the desperate, consuming hunger she'd experienced lately, but a softer desire for more connection, more closeness.

"Keith?" she ventured as his breathing began to steady.

"Hmm?" He nuzzled against her neck, clearly satisfied and drifting toward contentment.

"Do you think ...?" Sam hesitated, then pressed on. "Could you stay inside me a little longer? Maybe

... keep going?"

Keith lifted his head, surprise evident in his expression. They'd rarely continued after his climax — it had never been part of their routine.

"You didn't ...?" he asked, concern creasing his brow.

Sam stroked his cheek. "It's not about that. I just want to feel close to you a little longer."

Something shifted in Keith's eyes — understanding, perhaps, or recognition of a deeper need than physical release. He kissed her softly, then began to move within her once more. His body was still sensitive from his release, making his movements gentler, more deliberate than before. Sam sighed with contentment, her hands trailing down his back to rest at his hips, guiding him in a slow, circular motion that touched places inside her that had been neglected in their usual couplings.

"Like this?" Keith murmured, watching her face with newfound attentiveness.

"Just like that," she breathed, closing her eyes to focus on the sensation of fullness, of connection.

They moved together in perfect synchronicity, their bodies remembering a language they'd nearly forgotten. Keith's fingers interlaced with hers, pinning her hands gently beside her head as he continued his steady rhythm. The position wasn't about dominance but about anchoring them together, creating a circuit of shared intimacy.

Sam felt the pleasure building gradually — not the violent, frightening surge that had characterized her experiences with Ty, but a warm glow that spread outward from her center, suffusing her entire being. It was as if each cell in her body was slowly illuminated, one by one, with golden light.

"I see you," Keith whispered, his gaze never leaving hers. "I really see you, Sam."

Those simple words broke something open inside her. Tears welled in her eyes as the pleasure deepened, transforming into something that transcended the physical. This wasn't just about bodies moving together; this was about souls reconnecting.

Keith's movements grew more confident as he witnessed her response, his own arousal building again. His hands cupped her face with reverence, thumbs brushing away the tears that spilled down her temples.

"Keith," she breathed, his name a prayer on her lips. "Oh, Keith ..."

The climax, when it came, was nothing like the shattering explosions she'd experienced with Ty or the relentless mechanical assault of the vibrator. Instead, it was like sinking into a warm bath — a gentle submersion into pleasure that radiated outward in concentric circles, washing through her body in waves that seemed to carry her soul along with them.

She clung to Keith as they trembled together, his second release coinciding perfectly with her own. Their foreheads pressed together, breath mingling, heartbeats synchronizing in the aftermath of shared ecstasy.

This — this was what had been missing lately. Not the intensity, not the forbidden thrill, but the profound connection that made physical pleasure merely a vehicle for something far more significant.

"I love you," Keith murmured against her lips, his weight a welcome comfort above her.

"I love you, too," she replied, and meant it with every fiber of her being.

They remained joined for long minutes afterward, neither willing to break the spell that had enveloped them. When Keith finally rolled to his side, he kept her close, one arm draped protectively across her waist.

"That was ..." he began, searching for words.

"Different," Sam finished.

He smiled. "Yes. In a good way."

Sam traced lazy circles on Keith's chest, savoring the warm afterglow of their connection. But even as contentment settled over her, a persistent voice in her mind whispered that this perfect moment was built on deception. The changes in her body, the strange experiences with Ty — these weren't secrets she could keep forever, especially not from the man who had just shared such profound intimacy with her.

"Keith ..." she said, her voice catching slightly. "There's something I need to tell you."

14

Keith turned toward her, his expression open and relaxed. The vulnerability in his eyes made her chest ache.

"I haven't been ... completely honest with you lately." Sam pushed herself up into a sitting position, pulling the sheet across her chest in an unconscious gesture of protection. "Something's been happening to me — to us — and I can't keep it from you anymore."

Keith's brow furrowed as he sat up beside her. "What do you mean?"

Sam took a deep breath. "I met someone. A man who said he moved into the neighborhood, claimed he inherited a house from his uncle." The words tumbled out faster now, as if releasing pressure that had built up inside her. "His name is Ty Boxx. And I ... I've been with him."

Keith's face drained of color. He stared at her, unblinking, as if waiting for her to say it was a joke.

"Sexually," she clarified, though it was unnecessary. "More than once."

Keith pulled away from her, creating a small gulf between them on the bed. "You're telling me you've been cheating on me?" His voice was eerily calm, though his hands trembled slightly.

"Yes," Sam whispered, tears welling in her eyes.

"And I'm so sorry. I don't know what came over me. It was like I was under some kind of spell—"

"A 'spell'?" Keith's voice hardened. "That's your excuse? A 'spell'?"

"I know how it sounds," Sam said, reaching for his hand. To her surprise, he didn't pull away. "But Keith, there's more to it. Ever since I met him, strange things have been happening to me, to my body."

Keith drew a deep breath, then released it as he asked, "Strange how?"

"I'll get into that in a second. First off, Ty isn't quite ... normal. His semen has this ... this blue tint to it, Keith. He claimed it's some rare medical condition, but I researched it and found nothing."

Keith ran a hand through his hair, his scientific mind visibly struggling with her fantastical account. "Blue-tinted semen? Sam, that's not possible."

"I know what I saw," she insisted. "And I ran into Jessica at the pharmacy ..." Sam decided now was most certainly not the time to mention her pregnancy scare. "She told me there's no record of anyone named 'Ty Boxx' moving into this neighborhood — not from buying, and not from inheritance. He lied about where he lives."

Keith was quiet for a long moment. "Why are you telling me this now?" he finally asked.

Sam gestured to the space between them. "Because it just makes the whole situation all the more strange. I met him back in the alley, where he was soothing a feral cat. But if he doesn't live around here, what was he doing there? And ..." She paused, hesitant to hurt him further. But she was committed now. "After we ... after we have sex, he just leaves me. I mean, literally leaves me unconscious in my own home."

Keith's eyes widened. "Unconscious?"

Sam nodded, her cheeks burning with embarrassment. "The orgasms he gives me are so intense that I black out completely. When I wake up, sometimes hours later, he's gone without a word. No goodbye, no note, nothing. Just ... vanished."

"Jesus, Sam." Keith's expression was a mixture of hurt, concern, and something else — a doctor's clinical interest despite himself. "That's not normal. Passing out from orgasms isn't something that typically happens."

"I know." She twisted the sheet between her fingers. "The first time, I thought maybe it was just ... I don't know, that he was just that good. But it happened every single time. And when I come to, he's nowhere to be found."

Keith fell silent for another long moment. "Where does he go? Have you ever seen him leave?"

"Once," Sam said, the memory crystallizing. "Yesterday, after he slipped out while I was in a stupor, rather than unconscious again. I went to the window and saw him walking away — heading west, on foot."

"West?" Keith frowned. "But there are only a few houses that way. After that, there's not much of anything, except the old nature preserve. It's just protected wetlands for miles."

Sam nodded slowly. "Exactly. If he doesn't

actually live in our neighborhood like he claimed, where is he going? Like you said, there aren't many houses out that way, no apartments, nothing."

"Unless he's living in the preserve illegally?" Keith suggested. "Some kind of makeshift shelter?"

"But that doesn't make sense either," Sam countered. "He's always immaculately clean, and decently dressed. Not like someone living rough in the woods." She hesitated, then added, "And there's something else — that feral cat I first saw him with? On one of his visits, it showed up at our door right before he did. Almost like it was ... waiting for him. And when he arrived, it just wandered off." A new thought occurred to her. "And ... I might be wrong, but I think it scampered off to the west, too."

Keith stood up abruptly, pacing beside the bed. "This doesn't make any sense, Sam. You're talking about a strange man, with blue-tinted semen, who makes you pass out during sex, and then disappears, maybe going into a protected wildlife area. Do you realize how all this sounds?"

"I do," she admitted, "especially hearing it all out loud. If someone told me this story, I'd think they were making it up, or hallucinating." She reached for him again. After a moment's hesitation, he let her take his hand. "But my *body* has changed, too, Keith. My breasts are smaller but more sensitive. The calluses on my hands and feet are gone. And I ... I can orgasm so easily now, unnaturally easily."

Keith raised an eyebrow. "Like ... like when I gave you a foot massage."

Sam nodded, but also chuckled. "That was

nothing, trust me."

"So what are we talking about then?'

"I'll show you," Sam whispered, suddenly determined. She moved to the center of the bed, leaning back against the headboard. With deliberate slowness, she spread her legs wide, exposing herself completely to her husband's gaze. "Just watch, Keith. Don't touch me."

Keith's eyes widened, but he settled at the foot of the bed, his expression a mixture of confusion, hurt, and undeniable curiosity.

Sam took a deep breath and brought her hands to her transformed breasts. The moment her fingertips brushed across her nipples, electricity shot through her body. She gasped, her back arching slightly.

"This is what's happening to me," she explained, her voice already growing breathless as she circled her aureolas with feather-light touches. "I can — oh! — I can feel everything so intensely now."

Keith watched in astonishment as Sam's breathing quickened, her skin flushing pink from her chest upward. Her fingers pinched and rolled her nipples, which she just now realized had grown, not only slightly longer, but also somewhat thicker since her encounters with Ty.

"My God," Keith whispered as Sam's hips began to rock involuntarily, though nothing was touching her between her legs.

"It's building already," she moaned, her head falling back, eyes half-closed. "Just from this ... just from touching my breasts."

Her movements became more focused, more

deliberate as she squeezed and tugged at her nipples. The pleasure spiraled outward from her chest, racing along nerve pathways that seemed newly forged or enhanced. Keith leaned forward, fascinated despite himself as his wife's body responded to stimulation that had never affected her so dramatically before.

"Keith," she gasped, her thighs beginning to tremble. "See, it's happening — I can't stop, couldn't stop even if I—"

With a sharp cry, Sam's back arched completely off the bed. Her body convulsed in unmistakable release, muscles tensing and releasing in rhythmic waves as the orgasm washed through her. Unlike the earth-shattering climaxes Ty had given her, this one didn't steal her consciousness, but it was still far more intense than anything she'd experienced before meeting him.

As the tremors subsided, Sam collapsed against the pillows, her chest heaving. "That's never happened before," she panted. "Not before the changes."

Keith sat motionless, his medical mind visibly struggling to process what he'd just witnessed. "That's ... that's not physiologically normal, Sam."

"I know," she agreed, pulling herself upright. "And there's more. My breasts — look closer." She cupped them, offering them for his inspection. "The color around my nipples has changed a little, too."

Keith leaned forward, his clinical gaze taking precedence over his emotional turmoil. His eyes narrowed as he studied the subtle bluish tint that threaded through the natural pink of her areolas.

"Jesus," he breathed.

"Yeah."

"And this is ... this is *all* real. Not a joke, or something."

Sam shook her head. "Keith, I wouldn't joke about—"

"No, I didn't mean about ... about Ty. I meant, this." He gestured up and down her body. "The changes, the orgasms ... all completely real."

Sam nodded. "Yes."

Keith thought for a moment, then said, "Give me your foot." She did, and he inspected her soles. "Huh. You're right, your feet are softer than before, softer than when I massaged them."

His probing fingers felt good, a little too good. "Keith, uh ..."

He looked up, and realized what was happening ... and a strange look crept into his eyes.

"What?" she asked.

He smiled. "So ... if I just ..." Keith's thumb pressed firmly into the arch of her foot, a deliberate, circular motion that made Sam's breath catch. He watched her face with newfound fascination as her eyelids fluttered.

"Keith, what are you — oh!" Her words dissolved into a gasp as he dragged his knuckles along her instep, applying just enough pressure to send waves of sensation up her legs.

"I'm conducting an experiment," he murmured, his detachment belied by the intensity in his gaze. His fingers worked methodically, finding every sensitive point on her sole with unerring precision. "For science."

Sam clutched at the sheets, her head falling back as pleasure built with alarming speed. "This isn't fair," she panted, even as her hips began to rock involuntarily.

"Consider it payback," Keith replied, his voice low. He pressed his thumb into the ball of her foot while simultaneously massaging her soft arch with his other hand. The dual stimulation sent lightning bolts of pleasure straight to her core.

"Keith!" Sam cried out, her back arching as a gentler orgasm washed through her. It wasn't the intensity of her nipple-induced climax, but waves of warmth that radiated from her center, leaving her trembling and flushed.

As she came down from the peak, she found Keith staring at her with an expression that mingled fascination with something ... else.

"Wh-what ...?" she gasped.

Keith's fingers pressed more deliberately into her arch, making Sam gasp. A mischievous glint appeared in his eyes.

"I have an idea," he said, his voice dropping to a register she rarely heard. "Something we've never tried before."

Sam's pulse quickened in a way that reminded her of Ty's presence. "What is it?"

Keith stood, still holding her ankle. "Lie back," he instructed gently, "down this way."

She obeyed, pulling down a pillow for her head, curious and slightly nervous. Keith positioned himself at the end of the bed, then guided both her feet toward his groin.

"I want you to use these," he said, placing her soft soles against his rapidly hardening length. "Your feet are so sensitive now ... I want to see what happens."

Sam's eyes widened with understanding. "A *footjob*?" The term felt foreign on her tongue — something she'd heard of, of course, but never considered, certainly nothing Keith had ever requested.

"If you're willing to try," Keith said, his breathing already quickening.

Sam nodded, feeling a strange thrill at this new territory. She positioned her feet on either side of his shaft, creating a channel with her arches. The moment his hot skin pressed against her newly sensitive soles, twin jolts of pleasure shot up her legs.

"Oh!" she gasped, not expecting the sensation to be so intense.

Keith groaned as she began to slide her feet up and down his length, finding a rhythm that seemed to please them both. The dual stimulation was extraordinary — each stroke sent waves of sensation through her body while satisfying her desire to please him.

"God, Sam," Keith moaned, his hands gripping her ankles to guide her movements. "That feels incredible."

She watched in fascination as his cock slid between her feet, leaving traces of moisture that only enhanced the glide. The sight was unexpectedly erotic — Keith standing there, completely at her mercy, his face contorted with the pleasure she was giving him in this new way.

"Is this good?" she asked, increasing her pace slightly.

"Perfect," he gasped. "You have no idea ..."

But she did have an idea. Each stroke against her sensitive soles sent currents of pleasure straight to her core. Her inner muscles clenched rhythmically, responding to stimulation that should have been too distant to matter. Yet her transformed body translated every touch, every pressure point into direct arousal.

"Keith," she panted, "I can feel it, too. It's like ... like you're touching me everywhere."

His eyes widened with understanding, then darkened with renewed desire. "Show me," he commanded softly. "Show me what it does to you."

Sam's head fell back as she continued working her feet against him. Without conscious thought, her thighs spread wider, offering him a view of how wet she'd become just from this contact. Her breath came in short gasps now, her hips rolling slightly against nothing but air.

"You're close again, aren't you?" Keith marveled, his voice thick with desire.

Sam could only nod, her ability to form words lost in the overwhelming sensations. Keith's movements grew more urgent, his shaft sliding faster between her feet as his own release approached — even though they had just made love, twice in a row. The pressure built within them both simultaneously, their connection deeper than ever despite this unorthodox joining.

"Sam," Keith groaned, his fingers tightening around her ankles. "I'm going to—"

With a strangled cry, Keith's body tensed. He pulled her feet tighter against him as his release erupted in thick, powerful jets that splashed across her thighs, belly, and even reached the undersides of her breasts. The hot, viscous fluid painted her skin in glistening stripes, marking her in the most primal way.

The moment his seed touched her hypersensitive skin, something extraordinary happened. Each droplet seemed to burn with pleasure, tiny points of ecstasy igniting across her body. Sam gasped, her back arching off the bed as the sensation spread like wildfire through her nervous system.

"Oh God, Keith!" she cried, her body convulsing as an unexpected orgasm slammed through her. This climax was different — not centered in her core but distributed across her entire being, radiating outward from every point where his semen had landed. Her vision fractured into kaleidoscopic patterns, colors bleeding into one another as consciousness began to slip away.

The last thing she heard was Keith's voice, distant and growing alarmed: "Sam? Sam, are you okay?"

Then sensual, sexual darkness claimed her completely.

* * *

Sam floated in a midnight-blue void, weightless and formless. Time had no meaning here, but awareness remained — a detached, dreamlike consciousness observing without participating.

A voice reached her through the darkness, familiar yet strange. Not Keith's gentle tones, but Ty's resonant timbre, now layered with something inhuman beneath the surface.

"The process has begun," the voice intoned. "Your body transforms. Soon you will be ready."

Sam tried to respond, to ask what he meant, but found herself without a voice.

"He cannot give you what I can," Ty continued. "His seed is weak. Not like mine."

As in her previous dream — and she now recognized that this was a dream — she felt her belly swell. The swelling began at her center, a warm expansion that stretched outward with mesmerizing speed. Sam watched in wonder as her abdomen distended, growing rounder and fuller by the second. Unlike the previous dream, this time she could feel every millimeter of the transformation — the delicious tension of skin stretching, the sublime heaviness pulling at her lower back, the exquisite pressure against her internal organs as they shifted to accommodate what grew within.

"Beautiful," Ty's voice caressed her mind. "You were made for this."

Her hands moved to cradle the massive dome of her belly, now so large she appeared to be carrying multiple full-term babies. Beneath her fingers, she traced the intricate network of veins that mapped her stretched skin — cobalt blue pathways that pulsed with each heartbeat. Some veins had risen to the surface, creating ridges she could follow with her fingertips, each touch sending sparks of pleasure through her transformed body.

"Can you feel them?" Ty asked. "Three perfect lives, growing inside you."

She could. Beneath the taut skin, movement rippled — not the gentle flutter of human babies, but something more deliberate, more synchronized. The sensation was intensely erotic, each shift and turn resonating through her entire being.

As her belly continued to expand beyond what should have been physically possible, her breasts underwent their own metamorphosis. They swelled dramatically, filling with milk meant to nourish what grew within her. The weight of them pulled at her chest, heavy and full, but instead of discomfort, she felt only mounting arousal. Her nipples darkened further, the bluish tint spreading outward across the entirety of her breasts.

Sam looked down at herself, marveling at how her body had become a vessel, dominated by her enormous belly and swollen breasts. Her limbs seemed almost incidental now, mere appendages to the fertility goddess she had become. She was more belly and breasts than woman — and yet she had never felt more feminine, more powerful, more complete.

"You are perfection," Ty's voice resonated through her.

The pressure inside her intensified, not painful but overwhelming in its sensuality. Her stretched skin gleamed in the darkness, the blue veins pulsing faster now, carrying something that wasn't quite blood through her transformed body.

"Soon," Ty promised as he suddenly appeared before her, naked, his cock engorged. "I will return, to

make you like this, very soon."

But then both Sam and Ty were startled when a male hand slapped down onto Ty's shoulder. Ty turned...

"No," Keith told the man. "You won't."

15

"Sam!"

Sam's eyes flew open, her heart hammering against her ribs. Keith's worried face hovered above her, his hands gently cradling her shoulders.

"Hey, hey, you're okay," he soothed, his brow furrowed with concern. He seemed to be telling himself this as much as her.

Sam blinked rapidly, trying to grasp at the fragments of her dream that were already dissolving like morning mist. Something about Ty ... and Keith confronting him? The details slipped away before she could hold onto them.

"I ... what happened?" she mumbled, struggling to sit up.

"You had another orgasm and passed out," Keith explained, helping her into a sitting position. His hands were steady but his eyes betrayed his unease. "It was different this time though, from what you've told me. You weren't unconscious for long — maybe thirty seconds at most."

Sam touched her abdomen instinctively, half-expecting to find it swollen. It was flat, of course. Just a dream. Relief and an inexplicable disappointment mingled in her chest.

"That's ... good, I guess?" she offered weakly.

Keith sat beside her on the bed, his expression shifting from concern to determination. "God, Sam, this so isn't normal. *None* of this is normal." He gestured to the streaks of his semen, still wet on her skin. "The way you responded when I just ... I mean, you literally orgasmed and passed out from me ejaculating on you."

"I know," she commented. She started to reach for his semen, to touch it with her fingers, but she was afraid she might go off again.

"Sam ..." Keith said. "When I said this wasn't normal, I didn't just mean your new hypersexuality."

"I don't understand."

He placed his hand on his own chest. "I just found out that my wife, the love of my life, has been cheating on me with a total stranger ... and a few minutes later, I'm asking you to give me a footjob? A *footjob*, for God's sake! *I'm* not behaving normally, either."

As guilty as his words made her feel, she saw his point.

Keith continued, "And look at this ..."

He gestured downward with his eyes. Sam followed his gaze, and gasped.

"Yeah," Keith said. "I ejaculated twice while we made love, then I shot a massive load of semen all over you from a footjob ... and I *still* have an erection."

It took some willpower for Sam to pull her eyes away from his hard cock. "But ... why would you ...?" Then she remembered something that she should have told him before.

"What?" he asked.

"There's something else you need to know," Sam said, her voice dropping in discomfort. "After I had sex with Ty for the second time, there wasn't any ... aftermath. You know how usually there's cleanup involved? With him, that time, there wasn't."

Keith's brow furrowed. "What do you mean?"

"His bluish semen ... and, I'm sorry to say this, but that time there was a *lot* of it ... but it never leaked out of me afterward." Sam felt heat rising to her cheeks despite everything they'd just done together. "It was like my body absorbed it completely. Every drop. Like it just disappeared inside me."

Keith stared at her, his keen mind processing this information. "That doesn't make sense. Unless ..." His eyes widened. "There are certain animal species where females can absorb seminal fluid directly through vaginal tissues. But humans don't ..." He trailed off, running a hand through his hair. "It could be pheromones. Maybe something in his chemical makeup is triggering biological changes in you — altering your hormone levels, your sensitivity, maybe even your tissue permeability. And now you're creating your own pheromones, and they're affecting me now, too ..."

Sam tried to focus on his words, but her eyes kept drifting down to his persistent erection. The sight of it made her mouth water involuntarily. She licked her lips, a gesture Keith immediately noticed.

"Sam?" His voice sounded strained. "Are you listening?"

"I'm trying," she admitted, dragging her gaze back to his face with visible effort. "But I keep getting ... distracted."

Keith followed her gaze downward, then groaned. "This isn't right. We should both be terrified, calling doctors, hospitals, and maybe even the police about Ty. Instead, I can't stop thinking about being inside you again." His hands clenched into fists at his sides. "It's like there's a fog in my head whenever I look at you now. And it's getting stronger."

Sam felt it, too — the magnetic pull between them, growing stronger by the second. The rational part of her brain was screaming that they needed to focus on this bizarre situation, but her body had other ideas.

And now, she was pleased to note, even *now*, any deliberate thought of sex with Ty just didn't have the same "kick" it did before. Now she just wanted her husband ... but they needed to focus, talk about what to do next ...

Damn it.

"We need to clear our heads," she decided, sliding off the bed to kneel before him. "Maybe if we ... take care of this, we can think straight afterward."

"But ... we've done so much already, I don't see how—"

Before Keith could protest, she took him into her mouth, enveloping him in wet heat. He gasped, his hand instinctively moving to the back of her head.

"Sam ... maybe we shouldn't—" But his objection dissolved into a moan as she hollowed her cheeks, creating suction that made his thighs tremble.

Whatever resistance he might have offered crumbled beneath the onslaught of pleasure.

Sam worked him with singular focus, determined to bring him to completion quickly so they could return to the matter at hand. But as his taste filled her mouth, she found herself savoring the experience in a way she never had before. Keith's flavor was different from Ty's — milder, without that metallic undertone — but equally intoxicating in its own way.

Keith's breathing grew ragged as Sam worked her tongue along the underside of his shaft. She could feel him throbbing against her palate, his body tensing as he approached his peak.

"Sam, I'm close ... *again*," he warned, his fingers threading through her hair.

She doubled her efforts, bobbing her head faster, taking him deeper with each stroke. When he finally erupted with a strangled cry, Sam swallowed eagerly, her throat working to capture every drop. The taste flooded her senses — different from Ty's strange fluid, sure, but no less potent in its effect on her transformed body.

To her surprise, as Keith's release subsided, his erection didn't follow suit. He remained fully hard between her lips, his flesh hot and pulsing.

"Sam," Keith gasped, his voice strained, "that was amazing, but I ... I'm *really* sensitive now. You— Ah! You should ..."

She ignored his gentle attempt to pull away, instead tightening her grip on his thighs and taking him even deeper. A strangled sound escaped him — half protest, half pleasure — as she pushed past her gag reflex and enveloped him completely.

"Oh, *God!*" Keith cried out, his hands now gripping the edge of the mattress. "It's too much, I-I-I can't— can't take—"

Sam held him there, her nose pressed against his abdomen, feeling him twitch and pulse against the back of her throat. The oversensitivity that should have been uncomfortable for him seemed to transform into a new kind of pleasure. Keith's hips began to move involuntarily, tiny thrusts that he couldn't control.

"How?" he moaned, his head thrown back. "*How* is this—? I ... I shouldn't be *able* to— not again, not this soon—"

Sam felt a surge of power as she held him captive with her mouth. She swallowed around him, her throat muscles massaging his length. Keith's entire body went rigid.

"Sam!" he shouted, his voice breaking as another climax tore through him.

This time, his release shot directly down her throat, bypassing her taste buds entirely. She felt the warm pulses as he emptied himself straight into her stomach. Unlike his previous orgasms, this one seemed endless, his body producing impossible amounts of fluid that she had no choice but to swallow continuously.

When she finally released him, pulling back to catch her breath, Keith collapsed onto the bed, his chest heaving. His eyes were wide with shock and confusion.

"That was ..." he panted, "...impossible.

Physiologically impossible."

Sam wiped her mouth, a strange warmth spreading through her abdomen where his seed now resided. "Yeah, I know."

Keith struggled to sit up. "The human male refractory period doesn't work this way. And the volume!" He shook his head in disbelief. "I should be completely depleted after our previous rounds. Instead..." He looked down at himself, and seemed relieved that he was *finally* going flaccid.

Sam stood up, her legs wobbling slightly as she steadied herself against the edge of the bed. The warmth in her abdomen had spread throughout her body now, mingling with the lingering sensations from their encounter. Every nerve ending felt electrified, ready to respond to the slightest touch.

"Okay, seriously," she said firmly, more to herself than to Keith. "We're caught in a kind of feedback loop. The more we satisfy these urges, the stronger they seem to get."

Keith nodded, his expression clearing slightly as if a fog was lifting. "You're right. We need to break this cycle."

"Cold showers," Sam declared, crossing her arms over her stomach to avoid accidentally brushing against her sensitive nipples. "Separate cold showers, right now. Then we need to get dressed — not in anything remotely sexy— and figure out what the hell to do about Ty."

Keith ran his hands through his hair, nodding with renewed determination. "Cold shower. Right."

16

They separated to different bathrooms, Sam taking the guest shower while Keith used their master bath. The icy water was a shock to her system, making her gasp as it cascaded over her hypersensitive skin. She welcomed the discomfort, focusing on the cold rather than the residual arousal that still thrummed through her veins.

Ten minutes later, shivering but clearer-headed, Sam entered their bedroom wrapped in a towel. Keith had already dressed in jeans and a plain t-shirt, his hair still damp.

"Here," he said, opening a drawer and pulling out his baggiest sweatpants and a faded college sweatshirt. "These should help."

Sam nodded gratefully, dropping her towel and quickly pulling on the oversized clothes. The fabric hung loosely on her frame, completely concealing her curves. Keith's masculine scent enveloped her, comforting in its familiarity — and she would not allow herself to "associate" beyond that familiarity.

"Better," she said, rolling up the sleeves that hung past her fingertips. "I feel less like a walking sex bomb and more like ... well, like someone wearing their husband's old gym clothes."

Keith's mouth quirked in a small smile. "Not

exactly your most flattering look, but definitely the safest."

They moved to the kitchen, where Keith put on a pot of coffee. The smell of the brewing beans helped ground them further, bringing a sense of normalcy to the surreal situation.

"Before we get started," Keith stated as he set down their coffee mugs, "I need to say something."

Sam swallowed against her flare-up of nerves.

Keith continued, "I forgive you. No, I don't *like* that you've been having an affair — I don't like it one bit."

Sam closed her eyes and nodded.

"But," he went on, "I'm no longer scoffing about the 'spell' you felt you were under. I mean, no, I don't believe in *magic*, but something highly unusual is happening. He affected you, and you affected me. So ... I choose to believe that, if Ty didn't have this ... whatever this is that started the whole thing, I believe that you would not have cheated on me. Okay?"

"Okay," Sam said, sitting at the table and wrapping her hands around the steaming mug — the relief she felt was beyond belief. She wanted to go to him, to hug and kiss him in gratitude, but she remembered that they could not be trusted to leave it at that. Instead, she said, "Let's think this through logically. What do we actually know about Ty?"

Keith pulled out his phone and opened the notes app. "Let's make a list. First, he claims to have inherited a house in our neighborhood, but according to Jessica, that's not true."

"He has some kind of ... 'physical anomaly' that

causes his semen to have a bluish tint," Sam added, her cheeks coloring slightly despite their clinical approach.

Keith typed rapidly. "And your 'adsorbing' this bluish semen seems to have triggered physical changes in you."

"Definitely," Sam agreed. "Heightened sensitivity, smaller breasts with that bluish tint to my nipples, the disappearance of calluses on my hands and feet ..."

"And behavioral changes," Keith added. "Hypersexuality, blackouts during orgasm."

Sam nodded, wrapping her arms around herself. "And there's a cyclical effect — my changes somehow affected you, too."

"Right." Keith's jaw tightened. "So we've got someone with physiologically impossible attributes who's clearly lying about who he is and where he lives." Then he glanced over at the groceries he had brought inside, which felt like days ago rather than an hour or more. "And he interrupted our nice dinner."

Sam smirked at that, but then got serious again. "The real question about all of this is, why?" Sam leaned forward. "Why *me*? Why our neighborhood?"

Keith drummed his fingers on the table. "We need to find out where he actually goes when he leaves here. If we can track him to wherever he's staying ..."

"We might discover who he really is," Sam finished, a chill running down her spine.

"Exactly. Maybe then we can call the police — *if* we can figure out how to approach his 'crimes' from a legal standpoint." Keith pulled up a map on his phone. "You said he headed west, right? Toward the nature preserve?"

Sam nodded and shrugged together. "That's the only time I saw which direction he went."

"The preserve extends for about three miles before hitting the river." Keith zoomed in on the satellite view. "There's nothing out there except wilderness and protected wetlands, which we already— Hang on..."

Sam perked up. "What?"

Keith zoomed in some more. "There's ... I think there's an old building in there."

"Inside the nature preserve?"

"Yes." He turned the phone so that she could see for herself.

"Why would there be an old building? Doesn't that defeat the purpose of a 'nature' preserve?"

Keith clicked some more, then typed into a search engine. "Hang on, this is ringing some old bells. I think that's an old research facility, the 'Meridian Institute.' But I thought they demolished that so long ago, I forgot about it."

Sam leaned in closer, studying the satellite image. "The Meridian Institute? What did they research?"

Keith scrolled through his phone some more. "Sounds like it had to do with indigenous birds or something. But there was controversy years ago, and the facility was shut down due to environmental contamination concerns."

"But they never demolished the building ..." Sam murmured.

"Apparently not." Keith's expression hardened.

"Maybe that is where Ty was going. But why there? Why not just rent an apartment or something?"

Sam stood, pacing the kitchen. "We need to follow him. Next time he shows up, we track him back to this place."

"Whoa, hold on." Keith put his phone down. "I don't think confronting him directly is safe. Whatever's happening to your body — to both of us — it's clearly not natural. Who knows what changes *he* has gone through?"

Sam remembered that brief moment where she'd thought Ty's eyes had seemed almost reptilian, and shuddered. "Then what? We just wait for him to come back and do God knows what else to me?"

Keith considered for a moment. "No, of course not. But we need to be smart about this. Strategic. You know ... I still have my old binoculars in the upstairs closet. Are you sure that he'll be back?"

"Oh, yes. He'll be back, probably tomorrow morning." Sam thought to mention about how dissatisfied Ty had seemed after having to settle for finishing with anal sex last time, but decided that there was zero reason to rub Keith's face in that kind of detail.

"So we need a plan," Keith said, pushing back from the table and standing. "A way to make him think you're still interested, but not let things ... progress."

Sam nodded, thinking. "I could meet him at the door tomorrow, but tell him I'm not feeling well. Maybe pretend I'm having my period?"

Keith's expression was skeptical. "Based on what

you've told me, I don't think he'll be easily deterred. He might even see that as a challenge." He drummed his fingers on the counter. "We need something that will make him leave of his own accord, without suspecting we're onto him."

"What if ..." Sam's eyes lit up. "What if I acted completely normal, even eager to see him, but then ... then I mention wanting to take things further? Like, suggesting we go on an actual date, or asking about his place?"

Keith's face brightened. "That's it. Men like him, I'll bet they thrive on their secrecy, their 'freedom.' If you start pushing for more information, for a 'deeper connection' ..."

"He'll retreat," Sam finished. "He's been careful to keep everything purely physical. The moment I try to shift it toward something more meaningful ..."

"He'll make an excuse and leave," Keith concluded. "And then we follow him."

"You could leave for work as usual, but then park your car down the street — to the east. Once he's gone, I'll text you. You pick me up, and we'll follow him—"

"From a safe distance," Keith insisted. "Using the binoculars as much as possible."

"Exactly."

Keith nodded, then deflated a bit under second thoughts. "This *sounds* good, but ... part of me still thinks we should call the police."

"And tell them what?" Sam asked. "That my affair partner has blue-tinted semen and makes me pass out from orgasms? That we *think* he might be living illegally in an old, abandoned building in the nature preserve?"

Keith sighed, knowing she was right. "Fine. But we stay at a safe distance the whole time we follow him. If we see him actually entering the preserve, we start taking pictures with our phones. Maybe that would be enough of a violation to get the law interested."

"Okay, then," Sam nodded. "I think we have a plan."

Keith nodded back and smiled ...

... and as soon as their plan — such as it was — was agreed upon, when they no longer had that to focus on, Sam felt a familiar stirring between her legs.

Uh-oh.

"Dinner," she blurted. "We should make dinner."

Keith nodded again, but she noticed that his eyes were beginning to wander — her baggy clothing be damned.

To their credit, they did manage to make and enjoy their dinner together. But by the time they were ready for dessert, they were both wrestling with an entirely different kind of hunger.

"Keith ..." she whispered.

"Yeah?"

"We've been good, and we have an intense day ahead of us." She met his eyes. "I think we should ... 'blow off some steam.' What do you think?"

His answer was the step around the table and scoop her up into his arms.

In the bedroom, clothes flew off as they fell onto the mattress. Keith's sweatshirt caught on Sam's elbow, and he nearly tore it helping her free. His mouth found hers in a desperate kiss as he positioned himself between her thighs.

"Now," she gasped against his lips, "I need you inside me *right now*."

Keith entered her with a single thrust that made them both cry out.

I should be so sore, Sam thought in amazement. *With everything my poor pussy has been put through* just today …!

But she wanted more, damn it. *More*, and *not* from Ty — she wanted her husband, she wanted *Keith*, and she wanted him in some new way.

What could they do? Between her trysts with Ty and her experimentations, both alone and then for and with Keith …

Inspiration struck. Pushing Keith's torso back, just for a moment, Sam hooked her legs up and over his shoulders, opening herself completely to him. The position allowed him to penetrate impossibly deep, touching places within her that sent jolts of pleasure throughout her body.

Based on his smile, Keith had no objections.

"Lean forward," she urged breathlessly, her hands clutching at his back. "See how far I can bend."

Keith complied, gradually folding her body beneath him until his chest nearly touched her breasts, her knees alongside her ears. The position should have been painful, should have strained muscles and tendons to their breaking point, but Sam felt only a delicious stretch and overwhelming fullness.

"Oh, my God," Keith gasped, staring down at her in wonder. "You shouldn't be able to bend like this."

No question, Sam's flexibility had increased dramatically — another transformation she hadn't even discovered until this moment. Her body accommodated the extreme position with ease, as if her joints and ligaments had been reconfigured for this very purpose.

"Wait ... wait ..." Sam gasped.

"What? Are you okay? Does it hurt?"

"No, no, it feels *wonderful*. And I want more of it. Try this ..."

Careful not to separate, they scooted around so that Sam's head was practically hanging off the edge of the bed.

"Now what?" Keith panted, having difficulty holding back his passion.

"The mattress limited where my legs and feet could go before," she told him. "But I want you to *test* my limits. Push my legs further, go *deeper*, deeper than you ever have before."

One final glimpse of caution and unease passed over Keith's face ... and then his own primal urges took over.

Moving as though he intended to do some pushups, Keith placed his palms against the backs of Sam's heels, his fingers clutching her newly-soft soles. And, as requested, he began pushing her legs back as he renewed his thrusting into her vagina.

"Yes ... deeper," she moaned, her fingernails digging into his shoulders. She loved feeling so helpless under him, so physically vulnerable. "I can take more.

Stretch me. Go deeper ... *deeper* ..."

Keith pushed Sam's legs back with increasing force, his eyes widening as her limbs yielded beyond what should have been anatomically possible. Her feet passed the edge of the mattress, her calves trying to follow, her toes inching toward the floor in an impossible arc that defied human physiology.

"My God," Keith breathed, his thrusts slowly increasing in strength as he watched her body contort. "Your hips, your spine ... you're not in pain, are you?" It was less a question, more a confirmation of sexual astonishment.

Sam's head hung further off the bed, her hair cascading down, but she felt no pain — only a delicious, impossible stretch that opened her completely to him. Her hamstrings, which should have been screaming in protest, felt elastic and pliant.

"Don't stop," she gasped, gripping his forearms. "Please don't stop!"

Keith thrust into her harder and harder, each one driving impossibly deeper as Sam's position allowed him access beyond anything they'd ever experienced. The angle pressed his cock against spots inside her that triggered pleasure so intense her vision began to blur — not as though she were going to pass out already, pre-orgasm, but like her mind was simply having difficulty processing so much physical bliss at once.

"I can ... feel you ... everywhere," she cried, her back arching as far as it could. "It's like ... you're touching my *soul*!"

Inside, Keith pressed firmly against her cervix —

something not even Ty had managed, not to this degree. A lot of it was this open, contortionist's position, but it also felt almost like ...

"Sam ..." he gasped, barely able to speak. "I feel so ... it's like I'm ... like I'm harder than ever before ... *bigger* ..."

Sam felt it, too — Keith almost seemed to be expanding inside her, stretching her further with each thrust, slamming against her cervix with delicious force. The sensation should have been painful, but instead sent her hurtling toward yet another explosive climax.

"Don't stop," she begged, her body beginning to convulse around him. "*Don't - stop!*"

Keith didn't stop. Locked in this impossible position, her body contorted far beyond her normal limits, her cervix bowed under the relentless pressure, creating a sensation that sent lightning bolts of pleasure straight to her brain.

"Keith!" she screamed as the orgasm hit, more powerful than anything she'd experienced before — the incident with the vibrator had lasted longer, but this had more strength behind it. Her inner muscles clamped down on him, milking him with rhythmic pulses that seemed to draw his very essence deeper into her body.

"Sam, I— I—" Keith's words dissolved into a guttural moan as his release erupted inside her. His body went rigid, his cock pulsing with each powerful jet of semen. The volume was shocking yet again, filling her completely before overflowing down her upturned ass.

And unlike her encounters with Ty, Sam remained conscious the entire time. Her vision further blurred and fractured at the edges, but she stayed present, watching Keith's face transform with pleasure and astonishment.

As their shared climax subsided, Keith carefully pulled her legs toward him, helping her back onto the bed properly. They collapsed side by side, gasping for breath, their bodies slick with sweat.

"That was ..." Keith struggled to find words.

"Yeah ..." Sam agreed, her voice hoarse from screaming.

They lay in silence for several minutes, their breathing gradually returning to normal. Keith traced lazy patterns on her stomach, his expression thoughtful.

"I know I probably don't need to tell you this," he said. "But your body shouldn't be able to bend that way. Unless you spend a lifetime in the circus, the human spine and hip joints have natural limitations. What you just did should have been anatomically impossible."

"Yeah," Sam nodded, staring at the ceiling. Then she shrugged. "Add it to the list, I guess. Enhanced flexibility, right under 'blue-tinted nipples' and 'orgasmic feet.'"

Despite the gravity of their situation, Keith chuckled. The sound was so normal, so refreshingly human that Sam found herself laughing, too. For a moment, they were just Sam and Keith again, finding humor in absurdity.

But the moment passed as Keith's expression

sobered. "Whatever's happening to you — to *us*, really, because I'm pretty damned sure my cock grew bigger than normal just now — it's accelerating. The changes are coming faster now."

Sam nodded. "I know." She pushed herself upright, wincing slightly; despite her newfound flexibility, her muscles still felt the aftermath of their intense coupling. "Let's get some sleep. If we're lucky, tomorrow we'll learn something about Ty Boxx."

Keith grunted. Then, after a moment, he stroked her back and said, "I love you, Samantha."

She melted back into his arms. "I love you, too, Keith."

17

Sam jolted awake, her eyes snapping open in the darkness. The digital clock read 3:12 AM. Her body felt uncomfortably warm, sheets twisted around her legs from restless sleep. The bed beside her was empty.

She sat up, pushing damp hair from her forehead. After their latest round of intense, super-flexible lovemaking, they'd decided Keith should sleep in the guest room — a desperate attempt to maintain some control over their urges. "Distance," he'd said. "Just until morning." She'd reluctantly agreed.

Now something had woken her. A sound? She held her breath, listening.

There it was again — a soft grunt from down the hall, followed by a frustrated sigh.

Sam slipped from bed, pulling one of Keith's T-shirts over her naked body. The floor felt cool against her soft, sensitive feet as she padded toward the guest room. The door stood slightly ajar, but the bed was empty, covers thrown back.

Light spilled from beneath the adjoining bathroom door. Another muffled groan reached her ears.

She pushed the door open without knocking.

Keith sat on the toilet, his pajama bottoms pulled down to his knees. His hand moved frantically over his erection, his face contorted in frustration rather than pleasure. He looked up, startled and embarrassed when she appeared.

"Sam! I— I didn't want to wake you." His hand stilled but didn't release himself. "I woke up and couldn't go back to sleep." He glance down. "It won't go away."

She took in the scene — his reddened cock, the desperate look in his eyes, the tension in his shoulders. Despite their marathon evening of sex, he was painfully hard again, yet seemingly unable to find release.

"How long have you been at this?" she asked softly.

Keith's shoulders slumped. "Half an hour, maybe longer. I keep getting kind of close, but ..." He released his erection. "I think the changes we're experiencing are at war with my old 'normal.' I mean, you can see I'm hard as a rock, but that doesn't change how many orgasms I had over the course of the evening, how much semen I ejaculated ..." He sighed in frustration again. "Maybe I should just take another cold shower and try to ignore it."

Sam was torn. She, herself, was feeling reasonably under control, but she didn't know how much longer that would last if she stayed with him. And yet, she didn't want to leave him like this ...

What could they do, together, that would not send them off to the races all over again? She considered her options. What if they went a little off the beaten path, leaned into something sexy but not sexual? Easier said than done, the way her body had been lately.

On a whim, she crossed past him to sit on the edge of the tub. He looked at her, a quizzical look in his eyes.

"You've always liked my legs, right?"

He blinked in surprise. "Yeah, you know I do. I love your legs."

She nodded and smiled. "That's why I had electrolysis done after we got married. I know you like them smooth. And when I flex them like this ..."

She flexed her thighs, then lifted her left leg — the one next to him — and flexed her calf muscle.

Keith cleared his throat. "Samantha ... we really probably shouldn't—"

"Don't worry, this is not leading to sex. Not literally, anyway." She moved her left leg so that it rested on his naked thighs. "I remember when you used to bite me sometimes, just little love-bites, bite my legs ..."

Keith smirked. "You didn't seem to like it, so I stopped."

"Honestly," she confessed, "I didn't. Not really. I liked that *you* liked it, but it didn't do anything for me."

"But ...?"

"But that was before. Before these changes."

Keith cleared his throat. "What do you have in mind?"

Sam flexed her calf muscle again and rubbed it back and forth across his thighs. "Here's the deal: No sex — at least, no intercourse. I want you to hold my leg with one hand while you jerk off with the other. I

want you to bite me, bite my calf. Just love-bites —
no blood, no bruising, nothing too hard or painful.
And don't touch my foot! That would be cheating."

Keith looked down at her sexy leg, and his cock
throbbed visibly. "What about you?"

"I'm going to *try* not to touch myself in any way.
But since I can now cum from a foot massage — hell,
I can cum from giving a footjob! — I want to know if
your love-bites can make me cum, too. But after that,
after you finally ejaculate and I, hopefully, get
something out of it, too ... after that, back to separate
bedrooms. Agreed?"

Keith nodded without looking away from her leg
on his lap.

Sam flexed her calf again. "So what are you
waiting for?"

Keith's hands trembled as he wrapped his fingers
around her calf, his touch reverent yet hungry. He
lifted her leg, leaned forward, and pressed his lips to
the curve of her muscle.

"Like this?" he murmured, his eyes flicking up to
meet hers.

"Just do what feels right," Sam encouraged,
settling herself more comfortably on the edge of the
tub.

Keith's other hand moved to his shaft, stroking
slowly as he placed the first tentative bite just below
her knee. The sensation was gentle — teeth barely
grazing her skin — yet it sent an unexpected shiver up
her spine.

"More," she whispered.

He grew bolder, taking a more substantial bite of

her calf muscle, his teeth applying enough pressure to dimple her skin without hurting. The sensation was entirely new for Sam — not quite pain, not quite pleasure, but something hovering delightfully between the two.

"Mmm," Sam breathed, surprised at the warmth beginning to pool between her thighs. "That's ... interesting."

Keith's rhythm on his cock increased slightly as he continued to explore her leg with his mouth, alternating between gentle nibbles and more substantial bites. His jaw worked against her flesh, teeth gently chewing at her calf in a way that should have been strange but instead sent tingles racing across her skin.

"Your skin always tastes so good," he groaned, his words vibrating against her flesh. "I can't believe I ever stopped doing this."

Sam's breathing quickened as Keith found a particularly sensitive spot midway up her calf. When his teeth grazed it, a jolt of pure pleasure shot straight to her core, making her gasp.

"There," she urged as she flexed her muscle against his teeth. "Right there."

Keith focused on that spot, gently gnawing at her flesh while his hand worked faster between his legs. The dual sensation of his teeth and his hot breath against her skin created a rhythm that her body began to respond to instinctively. Her inner muscles clenched in time with each bite, building a tension that mounted with surprising speed.

"Keith," she panted, gripping the edge of the tub.

"I think I might actually—"

"Don't fight it," he urged, his voice husky with his own arousal. "Let it happen."

He dug in with his teeth a little harder, applying just enough pressure to intensify the sensation without crossing into pain. Sam's head fell back, her thighs trembling as pleasure radiated outward from where his mouth worked her calf.

"I never knew," she gasped. "Never knew this, *this*, could feel so— Ah!"

Keith's free hand tightened around her leg, holding her steady as his own arousal built. His cock throbbed visibly in his grip, pre-cum glistening at the tip as he stroked himself with increasing urgency.

"I think I'm finally getting close," he warned, his breathing ragged. "Sam ... I ..."

"Do it," she encouraged, lifting her other leg slightly higher, offering herself more completely to his hungry gaze. "Don't hold back."

Keith's teeth pressed even deeper into her calf— still not enough to actually cause damage, but hinting in that direction — as his hand worked frantically, his rhythm growing erratic. His muscles tensed, breath coming in harsh pants against her skin, but release still hovered just beyond his reach. The struggle was visible on his face — desperate need warring with physical limitations.

"I'm right there," he groaned, frustration evident in his strained voice. "So close ..."

Sam felt her own pleasure building to a crescendo, her body responding to the pressure of his teeth with mounting waves of sensation. She watched his face, the concentration in his eyes, the tension in his jaw as he continued to love-bite her leg while stroking himself.

"Look at me," she whispered, catching his gaze. "Don't look away."

Their eyes locked, creating a connection that transcended the physical. Something in that shared gaze finally pushed Keith over the edge. His back arched, a strangled cry escaping his throat as his release erupted in thick, pearlescent ropes across her other leg — a normal-sized load this time. The warm splash against her sensitive skin triggered Sam's own climax instantaneously — a sympathetic response that rocked through her body in perfect synchronicity with his.

"Ohhhhh!" she cried out, her thighs clenching as pleasure radiated outward from her core. No direct stimulation, just the warmth of his seed on her leg and the pressure of his teeth — yet her body convulsed in waves of ecstasy that left her gasping.

They remained frozen in that tableau for several heartbeats — Keith's mouth still against her calf, his release warm, then cooling on her other leg, both of them trembling with the aftershocks of shared pleasure.

Finally, Keith released her leg, falling back against the toilet tank with a dazed expression. "That was ... very different."

"You're telling me," Sam breathed.

After recovering for a minute, Keith reached for a washcloth. "Back to separate beds?"

Sam nodded reluctantly.

They shared one last, lingering kiss before Sam returned to their bedroom, her body still humming with residual pleasure.

18

Morning came too quickly, the alarm's insistent beeping pulling Sam from fitful dreams. She rolled over, surprised to find Keith already up, in their bedroom, and dressed in his work clothes. He turned to smile at her, and she noticed his phone pressed to his ear.

"Yes, I understand it's short notice," he was saying as he returned his gaze to looking out the bedroom window. "Family emergency. I'll need to reschedule all of today's appointments." He paused, listening. "Thank you, Melanie. I appreciate it."

Sam sat up, the sheet falling away. Keith turned, offering her a meaningful look as he continued his conversation.

"Yes, that's right. Tell Mrs. Hendricks I'm especially sorry about her lower back pain. I'll fit her in first thing tomorrow." He ended the call and set his phone down. "That's done. Everyone on staff thinks I'm dealing with a family emergency."

Sam nodded, her nerves fluttering at what was to come.

Keith adjusted his tie with practiced movements. "I'll leave like normal, park around the corner on Maple, and wait for your text." He crossed to the bed, leaning down to kiss her forehead. "Remember, keep him talking until he scampers. Don't let things ... progress."

"I know," she assured him, though her confidence wavered. Would she be able to resist if Ty's presence triggered that overwhelming desire again?

Keith grabbed his briefcase, hesitating at the bedroom door. "Be careful, Sam. If you feel unsafe, for even a second—"

"I'll call you right away," she promised.

After Keith left — closing the front door loudly for the benefit of any watching eyes — Sam showered in a rush and dressed in loose-fitting jeans and a buttoned blouse. Nothing provocative, but nothing that screamed "I'm trying to avoid sex" either.

She was rinsing her coffee mug in the sink when the doorbell rang.

Eighteen minutes. That's all it had taken after Keith's car pulled away.

Sam's pulse quickened as she moved to the door, forcing herself to take deep, steadying breaths. She could do this. Just talk to him, suggest a deeper relationship, watch him retreat.

The doorbell rang again, more insistent this time.

She pulled the door open to find Ty standing on her threshold, looking more disheveled than usual. His normally perfect hair was slightly mussed, as if he'd been running his hands through it. The blue of his eyes seemed more intense, almost luminous in the morning light.

"Took you long enough," he said without preamble, already stepping forward.

Sam blocked his path, one hand raised. "Actually,

I'm glad you're here. I've been wanting to talk."

Ty paused, his brow furrowing slightly. "Talk?" The word sounded distasteful on his tongue, as if the concept itself repulsed him.

"Yes," Sam insisted, gesturing toward the living room. "Please, come in. I made some coffee."

Ty's eyes narrowed, a flash of irritation crossing his features before he schooled them back to neutral. "We don't need to 'talk,' Sam. We both know why I'm here."

He stepped closer, his scent washing over her — that now-familiar blend of something spicy and metallic that made her nerve endings tingle. Sam swallowed hard, forcing herself to stand her ground.

"Actually, that's exactly what I want to discuss," she said, her voice steadier than she expected. "This ... thing between us. I feel like we've been dancing around it for days now."

Ty cocked his head, studying her with those unnaturally blue eyes. "Dancing around what, exactly?"

"Us," Sam said, gesturing between them. "What this means. Where it's going." She took a deliberate breath. "I don't even know where you live, Ty."

His posture stiffened. "I told you. The house at the far end—"

"Far end of the block," Sam finished. "Yes, I know what you said. But which house, exactly? I've lived in this neighborhood for years, and I don't recall any houses changing owners recently. Or any of my neighbors passing away, for that matter."

Ty's jaw tightened. He stepped past her into the

living room, but didn't sit. Instead, he paced like a caged animal.

"Why the sudden interest in my living arrangements?" he asked, his voice carrying a dangerous edge.

Sam leaned against the wall, maintaining distance between them. "Because I want to know more about you. About your life." She forced a shy smile. "Maybe I could come over sometime? Maybe we could ..." She forced herself to go on, injecting some false desire into her tone. "Maybe we could fuck over there for a change, you know? You've spent so much time here—"

"That won't be possible."

"Why not?"

"Renovations," he said smoothly, though his eyes had darkened. "The place is barely habitable. That's why I take so many walks."

"Then where have you been staying?" Sam pressed, watching his reaction carefully.

Ty's fingers flexed at his sides. "You're asking a lot of questions today, Samantha." Then he smiled, a predatory look on his face. "I can think of better uses for your mouth."

Sam glossed over that last part. "Is that so strange, to ask questions? We've been intimate for days now. I think it's natural to want to know more about the man I'm sleeping with."

Ty's expression darkened as his patience visibly snapped. With swift, deliberate movements, he unbuckled his belt and unzipped his pants.

"Enough questions," he growled, freeing his

already-hardened length. "*This* is what you really want. *This* is all you need to know about me."

He moved toward her with predaceous intent, one hand reaching to grip the back of her head. His fingers tangled in her hair, not painfully but with unmistakable dominance.

"On your knees," he commanded, his voice dropping to that hypnotic register that had so easily controlled her before.

Sam felt the familiar pull, that strange magnetic attraction that had drawn her to him from the beginning. Her body responded with a flush of warmth, her mouth watering involuntarily as she stared at his impressive erection. The bluish veins pulsed visibly beneath the surface, and for a moment, she swayed toward him.

But something was different now. The compulsion wasn't as overwhelming as before.

As she hesitated, her mind drifted unexpectedly to Keith — to his gentler touch, the way his eyes had locked with hers last night while he pleasured himself. She remembered the taste of him, how her husband had filled her mouth with such perfect consideration.

The realization hit her with startling clarity: It wasn't Ty's cock she wanted between her lips, anymore. It was Keith's. Deep down, it had always been Keith's — Keith's body, Keith's mind, Keith's love. Ty had just taken advantage of her listlessness.

"No," she said, the word emerging stronger than she anticipated. She stepped back, breaking his grip on her hair. "I'm not doing this. Not without answers *first*. I want more from you. I want a relationship."

She almost slipped and laughed at that last part — it sounded so fake to her ears, she hoped Ty couldn't detect the falsehood.

Ty's eyes flashed dangerously, a flicker of something inhuman passing through them. Had his pupils looked like vertical slits again? Had that been more than her imagination? With all the changes in her own body ...

"You've never refused before," he said, his voice carrying a strange, multi-toned quality she'd never noticed. "Never pushed for *more*. What's changed?"

Sam maintained her distance, edging toward the front door. "Maybe *I* have. Maybe I'm tired of being left unconscious while you disappear without a word."

Ty's nostrils flared as he tucked himself back into his pants, his movements jerky with frustration. "This isn't how this works, Samantha Darby." He gestured between them. "You need this. You need *me.*"

"Do I?" she challenged, finding unexpected strength in her resistance. "Because right now, I'm pretty damned sure I need *more* than I need whatever 'this' is."

His eyes narrowed as he studied her face, then swept down her body as if searching for something.

"You've been with him," he said flatly. "Your husband."

Sam didn't deny it. "He *is* my *husband.*"

Ty's lip curled in disgust. "And what did that accomplish? His seed is weak, ineffective. He can't give you what I can."

The words sent a chill down Sam's spine, echoing fragments of her strange dreams. "And what exactly is it you think you're giving—?"

Before Sam could finish her question, Ty's face contorted with rage. In two swift strides, he closed the distance between them, his hand shooting out to grasp her throat. His fingers didn't squeeze — not quite, not yet — but the threat was unmistakable as he backed her against the wall.

"You think this is a game?" he hissed, his face inches from hers. The blue of his eyes seemed to pulse with an internal light, and this time there was no mistaking it — his pupils had definitely narrowed into vertical slits, if only for another second or less. "You think *you* get to dictate terms?"

Sam's heart hammered against her ribs. The hand at her throat felt abnormally hot, almost burning against her skin. She could feel her pulse throbbing beneath his palm.

"Let go of me," she managed, her voice surprisingly steady despite her fear. "Now."

Something flickered across Ty's face — surprise, perhaps, that she wasn't cowering. His grip loosened slightly, and he tilted his head as if reassessing her.

"You *have* changed," he said, his voice dropping to a contemplative murmur, barely audible even this close. "Faster than expected, yet somehow—"

Sam pushed against his chest, and to her surprise, he stepped back, releasing her throat. She rubbed the tender skin where his fingers had been, watching warily as he paced a tight circle in her living room.

"Fine," he snapped suddenly, his tone shifting to cold dismissal. "Have it your way. Waste time with your pathetic husband. See if he can satisfy you, now." He gestured vaguely at her body. "But we both know you'll be begging for me soon enough."

He adjusted his clothing with sharp, angry movements. "I'll come back when you're ready to get serious about your physical needs. And trust me, Samantha — those needs will only grow more ... specific."

Without another word, he strode to the door, yanking it open with such force that it banged against the wall. The sound of his footsteps receded down the walkway, and then he was gone.

Sam remained frozen for several seconds, her breathing shallow. When she finally moved to the window, she watched Ty's retreating figure with a mixture of relief and dread. Just as she'd seen before, he was heading west — toward the nature preserve.

Her hands trembled slightly as she pulled out her phone and typed a quick message to Keith: *He's gone. Heading west again. Meet me in five.*

She watched until Ty disappeared from view, then grabbed her jacket and keys. Whatever he was hiding, wherever he was living — in the preserve? in that abandoned research facility? — they were going to find out.

The neighborhood seemed unnaturally quiet as Sam hurried down her front steps. No children playing, no neighbors working in their yards — just empty driveways and curtained windows. Had it always been this deserted on weekday mornings?

Keith's car appeared at the corner right on schedule, pulling up beside her with a soft purr of the engine. Sam slipped into the passenger seat, her heart still racing.

"Are you okay?" Keith asked immediately, his eyes scanning her face, then her throat where faint red marks remained.

"I'm fine," she assured him, though her voice sounded strained even to her own ears. "He got angry, but I'm okay. Drive — he's heading west on foot."

Keith pulled away from the curb, keeping their speed deliberately slow. "Did he hurt you?"

"Not really." Sam's fingers brushed the skin of her neck. "He grabbed my throat but didn't really squeeze. I think he was more surprised than anything when I refused him."

Keith's knuckles whitened on the steering wheel. "I should have been there."

"This was the plan," Sam reminded him. "And it worked — he left, without any sexual interaction between us. Now we follow."

They drove to the end of their street, then turned onto Hawthorn Drive, the road that eventually led right to the edge of the nature preserve.

"There he is!" Sam pointed.

Keith kept the car rolling at a leisurely pace, maintaining a significant distance behind Ty's striding figure.

"Here," Keith handed her the binoculars he'd retrieved from the glove compartment. "Keep an eye on him."

Sam raised the binoculars to her eyes, adjusting the focus. Ty came into sharp relief — his shoulders rigid with anger, his stride purposeful. She noticed something odd about his movements, a subtle but distinctive fluidity that seemed almost too graceful.

"He walks like a dancer," she murmured. "Or maybe a predator."

As they approached the official border to the preserve, they slowed further. The road curved around the perimeter, with a small parking area for hikers and bird watchers. But Ty didn't head for this spot — instead, he veered off the road before reaching it, disappearing into a thicket of underbrush where no clear opening existed.

"Stop here," Sam instructed. "We can't follow him by car anymore."

Keith pulled over to the curb, positioning their vehicle to face the parking area and the preserve. Through the binoculars, Sam could just barely make out Ty's form moving through the trees, heading deeper into the protected land.

"He's definitely gone into the preserve," she confirmed. "Away from any trails that I can see."

Keith reached for his phone. "I'm taking pictures. At a minimum, this is trespassing."

"Too late." Even using the binoculars, Ty had disappeared from sight just as the terrain turned marshy near the wetlands area — he had never hesitated or slowed.

"We need to follow him on foot," Sam said, already reaching for the door handle.

Keith caught her arm. "Last chance to back out of this."

Samantha met his gaze. "Do I look like a woman who's going to back down?"

Keith took in her demeanor, then nodded. He

leaned over and kissed her — a brief but emotional exchange. He had intended it for affection, and for luck ... but each of their bodies still reacted to it.

Keith groaned. "Damn it."

Sam leaned back, feeling the heat between her legs — at least she'd remembered to wear a padded bra, so that her nipples received minimal stimulation from the movement. "Yeah. Me, too."

Keith peered down at the obvious bulge in the crotch of his jeans. "We don't have time to do anything. Not now."

"No, we don't." She reached over and took his hand. When he looked at her, she told him, "After we're done, after we have enough evidence to be sure Ty gets arrested ... we'll go home, and I will ride your cock until we're both too exhausted to move. Okay?"

He groaned again at the effect her "dirty talk" had on him. But he said, "Okay. Let's go."

They got out of the car.

19

The preserve's terrain grew challenging almost immediately. What looked like manageable underbrush from the road quickly became a tangle of thorny brambles and ankle-twisting depressions. Sam pushed forward, ignoring the scratches forming on her forearms as she held branches away from her face.

"Any sign of him?" Keith whispered, close behind her.

"Nothing," she replied, frustration edging her voice. The muggy heat clung to her skin, dampening her blouse as they ventured deeper into the preserve.

They pressed on, the ground becoming increasingly marshy. Sam's sneakers sank into the soft earth with each step, making a wet sucking sound when she pulled them free. The canopy overhead thickened, dappling the forest floor with shifting patterns of light and shadow.

"We should have brought a compass," Keith muttered, wiping sweat from his brow. "Or at least marked our path somehow."

Sam paused, scanning their surroundings. The preserve had seemed much smaller on the map, but now it stretched in all directions, a labyrinth of identical-looking trees and vegetation. Her stomach tightened with the first tendrils of genuine fear.

"Maybe we should turn back," Keith suggested, his voice low. "We can call the police anonymously, report a possible trespassing—"

"Wait." Sam grabbed his arm, pointing through a break in the trees. "There's something over there."

They changed direction, pushing through a particularly dense thicket of undergrowth. The ground became firmer beneath their feet as they approached what appeared to be a man-made clearing. And there, rising from the midst of the wilderness like something from a forgotten era, stood a concrete structure, its gray façade stained with decades of weather and neglect.

"I think that's the old Meridian Institute," Keith breathed.

Like the preserve, the building was larger than Sam had expected from the satellite images — a sprawling single-story complex with several wings extending outward. Most of the windows were boarded up or broken, and thick vines crawled up the walls, nature slowly reclaiming what humans had abandoned.

"Look," Sam whispered, pointing to a side entrance where a heavy metal door stood slightly ajar. "Someone's been here recently. It has to've been Ty."

They approached cautiously, staying within the treeline for cover. The stillness around the building felt unnatural — no birds called, no insects buzzed. It was as if the wildlife instinctively avoided this place.

"I don't see him," Keith murmured, scanning the perimeter.

"He must have gone inside." Sam's voice was

barely audible. "We need to get closer."

Keith hesitated, his expression troubled. "I don't like this, Sam."

"We've come this far," she insisted. "We need to confirm this is where he's been squatting. Take some pictures, get proof, then we take it to the police."

They crept toward the building, every sense heightened. As they approached the ajar door, Sam's foot caught on an exposed root, sending her stumbling forward with a small cry. Keith caught her arm before she fell, both freezing in place as the sound seemed to echo unnaturally in the silence.

"Careful," Keith whispered, his grip tightening on her elbow.

They reached the metal door, its surface cool despite the humid air. Keith pushed it open a little wider, the hinges protesting with a low groan that made Sam's skin prickle. She peered into the darkness beyond, a corridor stretching ahead, lit only by thin shafts of light filtering through cracks in the boarded windows.

"Stay behind me," Keith murmured, pulling out his phone to use as a flashlight.

The beam cut through the gloom, revealing peeling paint and debris scattered across the floor. They stepped inside, the temperature dropping noticeably as they left the sunlight behind. Their footsteps echoed on the concrete despite their attempts to move quietly.

The corridor branched off in several directions, each hallway identical to the last — clinical, abandoned, eerie. Keith pointed to faint scuff marks on the dusty floor, signs that someone had passed this way recently.

They followed the marks, turning left, then right, moving deeper into the labyrinthine structure. The air grew thicker, heavier, carrying an odd tang that made Sam's nostrils flare. It reminded her of copper pennies left in the rain, or blood, but with an unfamiliar chemical undertone.

"Do you smell that?" she whispered.

Keith nodded, his face tense. "Metallic. And ... wrong somehow."

Sam's eyes widened when she realized that the smell reminded her, just a little, of the metallic smell that came off of Ty.

The scent grew stronger as they ventured further, until they reached a set of double doors at the end of a wide hallway. One door hung askew on its hinges, creating a gap just wide enough for them to slip through.

Beyond lay a cavernous space — what must have once been the main research area. Broken equipment lay scattered about, tables overturned, old bird cages discarded, ceiling panels dangling precariously overhead. A few dirty, leaf-covered skylights provided enough light to see by, allowing Keith to turn off his phone's flashlight.

The metallic smell was stronger here.

"I don't see him," Keith whispered, peering around the room.

Sam shook her head, scanning for any sign of Ty. Despite the obvious neglect, the room felt ... occupied somehow. As if someone had been here recently.

"Look at this," Keith said, moving toward a table that stood apart from the others. Unlike the dust-covered surfaces around it, this one appeared relatively clean. Several glass vials lay in a neat row, their contents a familiar cerulean blue.

Sam's heart skipped a beat. "That's the color. It's deeper, richer, but I think it's the same color as Ty's—"

A sound interrupted her — so faint she might have imagined it. She held up a hand, signaling Keith to silence. They stood motionless, straining to hear.

There it was again — a low moan, distinctly female, emanating from somewhere across the vast room. Sam and Keith exchanged alarmed glances.

"You heard that?" Sam whispered, her heart hammering against her ribs.

Keith nodded, his face pale in the dim light. "It sounded like—"

Another moan drifted through the air, followed by a second, different voice making a similar sound — weak and distressed. The sounds were barely audible, as if the women making them had little strength left.

"Someone else is here," Sam hissed, already moving toward the source of the sounds. "They might need help."

Keith gripped her arm. "Let's be very, very careful. We don't know *what* we're walking into."

They crept forward, weaving through overturned equipment and broken furniture. The moaning grew marginally louder as they approached a row of tall metal filing cabinets arranged in an L-shape at the far end of the room, creating a makeshift partition.

Sam peered around the edge of the cabinets and gasped, her hand flying to her mouth. Keith pushed forward to see what had shocked her, then froze beside her.

Two women lay on hospital-style gurneys, partially reclined. Their eyes were half-open but unfocused, gazing vacantly at nothing. But it was their appearance that sent ice through Sam's veins.

Their skin had a distinct blue tint — not the subtle shade of Sam's changing areolas, but a more pronounced cerulean that covered their entire bodies. Both women's abdomens were grotesquely distended, swollen far beyond what any normal pregnancy should be. They looked as though they were each carrying multiple full-term babies — triplets at least, maybe more.

"Oh my God," Keith breathed. "Wh-what ...?"

The woman closest to them turned her head slightly at the sound of Keith's voice. Her movements were sluggish, dreamlike. Up close, Sam could see the network of darker blue veins that mapped across her stretched belly, pulsing with each heartbeat. The sight was horrifyingly familiar — so like her dreams.

"Can you hear me?" Keith asked, keeping his voice low as he checked the first woman's pulse. "My name is Keith. I'm a ... I'm a doctor. We're going to get you help."

The woman's lips parted, but only another soft moan emerged. Her eyes, Sam noticed with growing horror, had the same vertical-slit pupils she'd glimpsed in Ty's.

"Keith," Sam whispered urgently, "look at her

eyes."

He glanced up, his expression hardening as he noticed the inhuman feature. "What the hell's going on here?"

The second woman stirred, her massively swollen belly shifting as something — or several somethings — moved beneath the taut, blue-tinged skin. Her hands, resting at her sides, sported fingernails that were entirely blue, like the fluid they had seen. The second woman made a cooing sound — Sam could not decide if it was a sound of pain, or desire.

The first woman suddenly reached out and latched onto Keith's wrist.

"Fff ... fff ..." she breathed.

Keith leaned closer. "Are you trying to speak?"

"Fffu ... fffu ..."

"What?"

The woman's strange eyes widened. "Fffuck me ... fffuck me, pleeease ..."

Keith jerked backward, but the woman's fingers clamped around his wrist with alarming strength. Her grip was like iron, all the more shocking coming from someone who appeared so weakened. He strained against her hold, his face contorting with effort.

"Let go!" he hissed, pushing against the gurney's base for leverage. Sam grabbed his other arm, adding her strength to his struggle. "She's so strong," he gasped. "How is she this strong?"

The woman's vacant expression transformed, shifting into an expression of undeniable longing. "*Need* it ... need *cock* ... please ... inside me..." Her free hand slid over her distended abdomen, caressing the taut skin with unsettling tenderness.

Meanwhile, the second woman began sluggishly writhing on her gurney, her hips lifting and falling in a rhythmic motion despite the enormous weight of her belly. Soft whimpers escaped her throat as she thrust upward against nothing, her hands clutching desperately at the thin mattress beneath her.

With a final desperate yank, Keith finally broke free, stumbling backward into Sam.

They retreated several steps, keeping their eyes fixed on the women. The first one reached toward them plaintively, her fingers grasping at the air. "Come back ... *fill* me ... need *more* ..."

"Keith," Sam breathed, her voice quavering. "This is what Ty was planning for *me*."

The realization crashed over her like ice water. The dreams, the physical changes, the insatiable desire — all of it had been preparation. These women were her future, if Ty had his way.

"We need to call for help," Keith said, fumbling for his phone. "These women need medical attention, and the police need to—"

A blur of motion from behind a toppled filing cabinet sent them both spinning around. A third woman lunged at them, her movements unnaturally quick and fluid. Her belly was smaller than the others', but still prominently rounded, the outline of multiple shapes visible beneath her stretched, blue-tinged skin.

The third woman slammed into Sam with shocking force, knocking her to the ground. The impact drove the air from Sam's lungs as the woman straddled her, pinning her with inhuman strength. Up close, the woman seemed to be in an earlier stage of the mysterious metamorphosis — her skin a lighter shade of blue, her pupils not fully vertical slits but elongated ovals.

"He chose *me!*" the woman hissed, her face inches from Sam's. Her fingers dug into Sam's shoulders with bruising force. "I can smell it on you! You're trying to take my place!"

Keith lunged forward, grabbing the woman's arm. "Get off her!"

The woman's head snapped toward him, her expression instantly transforming from rage to desire. She released one of Sam's shoulders to stroke Keith's face with disturbing gentleness.

"You ..." she purred, her body undulating sinuously despite her pregnant state. Her nostrils flared as she inhaled deeply. "*You* could fill me ..."

Sam took advantage of the distraction, bucking her hips and twisting sideways. The woman hissed, her attention returning to Sam with renewed fury. She bent backward at an impossible angle, her spine flexing like a contortionist's as she maintained her grip on Sam while simultaneously pressing against Keith.

Satisfied that Sam was still her captive, she focused on Keith. Her free hand slid down to caress her swollen belly. "They're hungry. Always so *hungry.*" She tried to smile, but it looked deranged. "I *need* you ... need to be *satisfied,* so they calm down ..."

Keith grabbed a broken piece of equipment from the floor and swung it at the woman's shoulder. She twisted away with serpentine grace, her body bending at angles that defied human anatomy. The blow glanced off her arm, barely affecting her.

"Please," the woman begged, reaching for Keith's belt. "Just a taste. Just a little of your *seed*."

Sam scrambled backward as the woman's grip loosened, her body sliding across the filthy concrete floor. Again the woman shifted focus, forgetting Keith and lunging toward Sam again with predatory focus.

Sam's back hit a metal cabinet. Trapped!

The woman advanced, her movements a disturbing combination of aggression and seduction. Behind her, Keith grabbed a fire extinguisher from a wall mount.

"Sam, duck!" he shouted.

Sam dropped to the floor as Keith swung the fire extinguisher with all his might. It connected with the back of the woman's head with a sickening thud. She staggered forward, her inhuman grace momentarily disrupted, then crumpled — she curled around her belly in a protective position before hitting the floor.

"Run!" Keith grabbed Sam's hand, yanking her to her feet.

They sprinted back toward the entrance, navigating the maze of overturned tables and broken equipment. Behind them, the moans of the other women grew louder, more desperate, as if they sensed the desired male escaping.

"Wait!" Sam hissed, skidding to a halt when she

spied the table with the blue vials. "Evidence. We need *proof*."

Keith hesitated for only a second before nodding.

Sam took all of one step toward the vials when the table was suddenly upturned ...

... by Ty Boxx.

20

Keith moved forward, instinctively pushing Sam behind him.

"Well, well." Ty was mostly in shadow, but his voice dripped with snark. "The concerned husband comes to the rescue. How noble. How ... inconvenient."

"Stay back," Keith warned, his voice steadier than Sam expected.

Ty laughed, the sound resonant in the confined space. "Or what, Keith Darby? You'll hit me with another fire extinguisher?" His head tilted, nostrils flaring. "I can smell her on you. The changes have begun. What a waste."

Ty took a step closer, and Sam then saw his face clearly. His skin had a subtle blue undertone, barely perceptible unless you knew what to look for. His eyes, however, were unmistakably changed — the pupils fully transformed into vertical slits, like a reptile's, like the pregnant women's.

"Jesus," Keith whispered. Then he demanded, "What the hell *are* you?"

"The future," Ty replied. His gaze shifted to Sam, hunger evident in his alien eyes. "And *she* is part of it. Her body is already adapting, preparing. Soon she'll be ready to receive my offspring."

Sam's hand instinctively went to her abdomen, revulsion washing through her. "These women ... that's what you planned for me. Isn't it?"

Ty shrugged. "They were just practice. Imperfect vessels. *You* are different. Your genetic compatibility is ... *exceptional.*

"I know you must've felt the changes by now — your heightened sensitivity, your flexibility, your body's capacity for pleasure beyond human limits." He remained where he stood, but his presence seemed to fill the large room. "That's just the beginning, Samantha. Imagine what comes *next.*"

The air between them grew thick with something like static electricity. Sam's skin prickled as memories of overwhelming pleasure flickered through her mind. Keith trembled beside her, as though he, too, were feeling ... *something* from Ty's voice.

"You were made for this, Samantha," Ty insisted, echoing her dreams. "To be transformed, to carry superior life. Your body craves it already." He gestured toward the other women. "They were nothing, just prototypes. *You* ... you'll be perfect — you'll carry multiple broods, each more advanced than the last." He smiled, his strange eyes glistening. "The pleasure you've experienced is *nothing* compared to what awaits you."

Sam felt it then — a strange flutter of consideration, a momentary curiosity about what such a transformation might feel like. Her body remembered the ecstasy Ty had given her, the impossible sensations. For one terrible moment, she imagined herself swollen with his offspring, skin tinged blue, lost in endless waves of pleasure ...

The image shattered as Keith's warm hand found hers, grounding her. His touch was solid, human, real.

"You're wrong," Sam said, her voice growing stronger with each word. "I don't want that. And I don't want *you*." She straightened her spine, stepping up beside Keith rather than behind him. "Keith is twice the man you'll ever be. He doesn't need to drug women or transform them into incubators to feel powerful."

Ty's face contorted with rage. "Don't be *absurd*. That pathetic human? He can't give you what I can!"

"You're right," Sam agreed, squeezing Keith's hand. "He gives me *more*. Love. Partnership. Respect." She met Ty's strange gaze unflinchingly. "Things you obviously couldn't understand."

Keith spoke up, his voice steady. "We're leaving now, but we'll be back for those women. They need help."

Ty's mouth stretched into something too wide to be a human smile. "I'm afraid that won't be possible. You see, the process is too far along for them. Their transformation is irreversible. And as for your departure ..."

Ty rushed toward them with blinding speed — before Sam realized what was happening, he had shoved Keith away and taken her by the shoulders.

"I've invested too much in you, Samantha," he hissed, his voice sounding less familiar with every passing second. "Your genetics are ideal. Your body is ready — *you* are ready!"

Sam felt a surge of anger rise within her, hot and

electric. Without thinking, she grabbed Ty's wrists and wrenched them away from her shoulders with a strength that surprised them both.

"Keep your hands *off* me!" she snarled, shoving him away.

Ty stumbled backward — actually stumbled — his eyes widening with shock as he regained his balance. "What the—?"

Sam looked down at her hands in momentary disbelief. The force she'd just used should have been impossible for a woman of her frame against a man of his build. Yet Ty had moved, had yielded to her strength.

"You didn't tell me everything about these changes, did you?" she said, a dangerous smile spreading across her face.

Ty's expression darkened, the blue of his eyes intensifying. "It doesn't matter," he spat. "You're still no match for—"

Sam didn't let him finish. She lunged forward, driving her shoulder into his midsection. The impact sent him crashing into a metal cabinet, denting the surface. Her muscles responded with a fluid power she'd never possessed before, her body moving with newfound grace and force.

During this, Keith had scrambled to his feet from where Ty shoved him. Now he grabbed a broken metal rod from the debris and swung it at Ty's legs.

Ty hissed — an actual hiss, not a human sound at all — and kicked the rod away, sending Keith sprawling again. But the distraction gave Sam the opening she needed.

She seized Ty by his shirt collar and slammed him against the wall. Plaster cracked behind his head. "Not so fun when the prey fights back, is it?"

Ty's face contorted, his features shifting subtly. The angles of his jawline became too sharp, his skin taking on a more pronounced blue tint. When he opened his mouth to snarl, Sam glimpsed teeth that seemed longer, more pointed than before.

"You think because you've absorbed some of my essence that you're my equal?" he spat, his voice carrying an underlying vibration that made the air hum. "You're nothing but a *vessel*!"

He broke her grip with a violent twist and struck out, his hand moving in a blur. Sam rolled with the punch with reflexes she didn't know she possessed, the blow grazing her cheek instead of connecting fully. But even that glancing touch stung like fire.

Keith charged again, throwing his full weight against Ty's side. Ty barely budged, casually backhanding Keith with enough force to send him tumbling across the floor all over again.

"Keith!" Sam cried out, seeing blood erupt from his nose.

"I'm okay," Keith gasped, pushing himself to his knees. "Keep fighting!"

Ty laughed, the sound resonating at a frequency that made Sam's teeth ache. "How touching. The weak male still tries to protect what's *mine*."

"I'm not yours," Sam growled, circling Ty warily. "I never was. You were nothing more than a *mistake*, a diversion I don't need anymore — and will never need again!"

She feinted left, then drove her fist toward his face. Ty blocked her with alarming speed, but Sam twisted her body in a way that should have been anatomically impossible, her spine bending like liquid as she dropped beneath his guard and swept his legs out from under him.

Ty crashed to the floor with a snarl but was on his feet again almost instantly. His movements became less human with each passing second, his limbs elongating slightly, joints bending at unnatural angles. The transformation was subtle but unmistakable.

Whatever Ty truly was, he wasn't human.

"You're fast," he hissed, circling her. "But I'm *stronger*. I've had decades to perfect this form."

He lunged forward, both hands outstretched like claws. Sam felt time slow as her body responded instinctively. She arched backward, her spine curving into a perfect bridge as his hands passed harmlessly above her. Without pausing, she continued the motion, flipping up and over to land in a crouch behind him.

"What—?" Ty spun around, genuine surprise flickering across his increasingly inhuman features.

Sam didn't waste the opening. She sprang upward, wrapping her legs around his torso while simultaneously twisting her upper body around his arms, locking them in place. The position defied normal human limitations, her body contorting like a gymnast and a snake combined.

Ty roared in frustration, trying to shake her off. He slammed her against a wall, pain exploding across her back. But Sam held on, her legs tightening around his midsection while her arms maintained their grip on his locked limbs.

"Get off me!" he snarled, his voice now carrying multiple tones layered beneath the human one.

Sam twisted her body further, using her newfound flexibility to wrap herself completely around him like a constrictor. She bent her neck at an impossible angle, bringing her face close to his.

"Looks like you wanted me flexible," she whispered, "but you didn't think about what *I* could do with it."

With a final, impossible contortion, she wrenched his arms backward at a sharp angle no joint could withstand. A sickening crack echoed through the room as something in Ty's shoulders gave way. He howled — a sound too alien to have come from human vocal cords.

Maintaining her advantage, Sam unwound herself from his body and kicked him squarely in the chest, sending him staggering into a tangle of broken equipment.

She landed in a crouch, her body humming with power and strange new awareness. As Ty struggled to rise, Sam — with a fluid movement that felt both alien and natural — sprang forward, seizing his head between her hands. A cold clarity filled her mind as she twisted sharply, applying force with precision she shouldn't possess.

The crack resonated through her palms, up her arms, and into her chest.

Final, definitive.

Ty's body convulsed once, then went limp, collapsing to the concrete floor with a dull thud. His eyes — those strange, reptilian slits — remained open, but the unnatural glow had faded, leaving only vacant blue orbs staring at nothing.

Sam stumbled backward, staring at her hands. They looked normal — her hands, her fingers — yet they had just snapped a man's neck with terrifying ease. She felt her legs weaken as the reality of what she'd done crashed over her.

"I killed him," she gasped. "I just ... I just *killed* someone."

Then Keith was at her side, pulling her into his arms despite his own injuries. Blood still trickled from his nose, and bruises were forming along his jaw. "You had no choice," he murmured into her hair. "He would have killed us both — or *worse*, for you."

Sam's body trembled, but not from remorse or horror. It was more like aftershocks — power still surging through her transformed muscles, her changed nervous system still firing with unnatural strength and coordination.

"I know," she said, pulling back to look into Keith's eyes. Her voice was steadier than she expected. "I know I had no choice. What scares me is how *easily* I did it. How ... *right* it felt." She looked back at Ty's body, noticing now that the blue tinge to his skin was deepening, spreading visibly across his face and hands. "Keith, he wasn't *human*."

"No," Keith agreed, "he was something else entirely."

A low moan from across the room reminded them

they weren't alone. The pregnant women were still there, still trapped in whatever transformation Ty had begun.

"What do we do now?" Sam asked, gesturing toward the women. "We can't just leave them here, but we can't exactly call 9-1-1 either. 'Hello, we've got three overly-pregnant blue-skinned women and a dead alien, please send help?'"

Keith ran a hand through his hair, wincing as he accidentally touched a bruised spot. "I ... I don't—"

A blinding flash erupted from the ceiling, bathing the room in harsh blue-white radiance. Sam's limbs locked mid-motion, her muscles seizing in sudden paralysis. Beside her, Keith froze in an awkward position, his mouth open in a silent cry.

The light intensified, pouring through cracks in the damaged ceiling that Sam hadn't noticed before. Dust particles suspended in the air glittered like microscopic stars as the concrete above them seemed to dissolve rather than break.

Two figures descended through the opening, their movements graceful despite their massive size, touching down on either side of Ty's body.

Sam could only watch, trapped in her own immobile body. The beings towered at least seven feet tall, their bodies sleek and powerful with pronounced musculature beneath skin that shimmered with iridescent blue scales. Their heads were elongated, with crests running from forehead to neck, and their faces bore only the vaguest resemblance to anything human — vertical-slit pupils dominated large, almond-shaped eyes that glowed with internal light.

Where Ty had shown hints of something inhuman beneath his disguise, these creatures were the fully realized form.

The taller one produced a slim, cylindrical device from somewhere within its scaled body. It emitted a soft humming as the being passed it over Ty's corpse. The device projected holographic symbols that floated and shifted in the air — a language or code Sam couldn't begin to comprehend.

The second being turned toward Sam and Keith, its movements deliberate and clinical. It approached them with the same scanning device, bathing first Keith then Sam in a grid of light that seemed to penetrate flesh and bone. Though she couldn't move, Sam could still feel — the scan sent waves of peculiar sensation rippling throughout her body.

The beings communicated with one another in harmonic tones that vibrated through Sam's skull, bypassing her ears entirely.

Then the first, taller being motioned toward the pregnant women, its elongated head tilting in an almost curious manner. It strode smoothly, almost gliding, across the debris-strewn floor, scanning each woman methodically. The blue light washing over their distended bellies caused rippling movements beneath their skin, as if whatever grew inside them responded to the energy.

Meanwhile, the second being remained fixated on Sam. Her heart hammered against her ribs, the only movement her frozen body could manage. The creature extended one massive, scaled hand toward her abdomen, its touch surprisingly gentle as it splayed long fingers across her stomach. The contact sent waves of warmth radiating through her core — not sexual, but something primordial, as if it were communicating directly with her cells.

Sam wanted to scream, to pull away, but remained locked in place as the being's glowing eyes studied her with clinical intensity. After what felt like an eternity, it withdrew its hand and turned away, moving with purpose toward the scattered vials of blue liquid. With elegant efficiency, it gathered each container, securing them within some unseen compartment in its scaled body.

The taller being made a series of harmonic tones that vibrated through the air. Both creatures positioned themselves equidistance between Ty's corpse and the three pregnant women. The blue-white light intensified, becoming almost unbearable to witness. Sam felt pressure building in her ears as the light coalesced around the beings, the women, and Ty's body. In a silent implosion of brilliance, they rose upward — not floating but simply ceasing to exist in one space and beginning to exist in another, higher one.

Then came darkness, followed by a final pulse of light that released Sam and Keith from their paralysis. They collapsed to the floor, gasping as control returned to their limbs.

"Wha— what ... just happened?" Keith sputtered, pushing himself to his hands and knees.

Sam scrambled to her feet, rushing to where the pregnant women had been. Nothing remained — not a trace of their presence, not even indentations on the gurneys where their considerable weight had rested. The same went for the one who had been curled up on the floor.

"They're gone," she whispered, her voice cracking. "All of them."

Keith staggered upright, wincing at his injuries. "The ceiling," he said, pointing upward. "Look at the ceiling."

Sam followed his gaze. Where there should have been a gaping hole from the beings' entrance, the concrete remained intact — aged and cracked, but unbroken. No evidence of their arrival or departure existed.

"That's impossible," she breathed. "We both saw it open up."

Keith moved to her side, wrapping an arm around her waist for support — though whether he was supporting her or himself remained unclear. "Let's get the hell out of here."

Sam offered no argument.

Together, they stumbled through the abandoned facility, and back to what they thought of as the real world.

EPILOGUE

Samantha arched her back as Keith drove into her with amazing force. Her ankles locked behind his neck, her thighs trembled as he penetrated impossibly deep. The position would have been excruciating for most normal woman, but Sam's remaining flexibility allowed her to open completely to him, her body receiving his enhanced size with ecstatic abandon.

"God, yes!" she cried, her fingernails leaving crescent marks on his shoulders. "Deeper! *Deeper!*"

Keith growled in response, his eyes heavy with primal hunger as he leaned forward, folding her nearly in half. The new girth of his cock stretched her deliciously, reaching places inside her that sent cascading waves of pleasure through her nervous system. The headboard slammed rhythmically against the wall, the sturdy bed frame creaking under their intensity.

"Yes, just like that," Sam gasped, her inner muscles clenching around him. "Don't stop ... don't *ever* stop ...!"

Keith shifted his angle slightly, the head of his cock pressing directly against her cervix. The sensation made Sam cry out, her vision blurring at the edges as pleasure built to nearly unbearable levels.

"I'm close," she moaned, feeling the familiar

tightening deep in her core. "So *close* ..."

Time had passed since their unbelievable experience with Ty, the pregnant women, and whatever those strange beings were. They had never reported any of it to anyone — with no remaining physical evidence, who would have believed them?

In the months that followed, the changes that Ty had affected upon Sam had regressed — somewhat. Sam's breasts returned to their normal size and color, and the skin on the soles of her feet and the fingers of her painting hand were toughening back up — though her feet remained soft enough to entice Keith to other activities, from time to time. She was also no longer stronger or inhumanly flexible, though she could still give the average gymnast a run for her money — most impressive, considering that she never had one minute of training, not so much as a yoga class.

But other elements remained potent still, and truth be told, they were hard pressed to complain about them.

While Sam could no longer achieve orgasm from a simple foot massage, her heightened sexual sensitivity did remain at least eighty percent of what it had been after Ty's alterations to her — likewise for sex drive, which had already been fairly strong.

Speaking of likewise, the changes in Keith seemed more or less permanent — so far, anyway. He was far more amorous than his old self, and his cock held onto its newer size, its length and girth noticeably enhanced from before. That, plus his increased semen production and his shortened refractory period ...

"Cum for me," Keith commanded, his thrusts

becoming even more forceful, more deliberate. His hands gripped her thighs, holding her in place as he drove into her with relentless precision.

The orgasm hit like a tidal wave, crashing through her body with such intensity that she screamed his name. Her inner walls pulsed around him, drawing him deeper as waves of ecstasy radiated outward from her center. Unlike before, she remained fully conscious through the peak, experiencing every exquisite second.

Yes, they couldn't deny they were enjoying the benefits of the changes in them. One could almost consider it their reward for surviving those events with their marriage intact and stronger than ever — not to mention their *lives*.

And there was one more, notable change since their shared, impossible experience, and it was one neither of them could have foreseen, perhaps the one they would have least expected, considering:

Sam and Keith had developed a mutual *breeding kink*.

Yes, they had tried for a baby for years, and yes, they would still love to have children someday. But before, it had been all about love, gentleness, and expansion of family. Now ...

"I'm almost there," Keith's voice grew ragged, his rhythm becoming urgent. His eyes locked with hers, darkening with primal intensity. "You know what I'm going to do to you, don't you?"

Sam nodded frantically, her body still quivering from her first climax. "Tell me," she insisted.

"I'm going to fill you so deep," he growled, his

words punctuating each powerful thrust. "Going to pump you full of my seed until it takes root inside you." His grip tightened on her thighs, pushing them wider. "Not just one baby, Sam. You're going to be swollen with twins, maybe triplets. Maybe *more*."

Sam moaned, feeling another orgasm building impossibly fast as his words penetrated her mind as deeply as his cock stretched her body.

"You'll be so beautiful," Keith continued, his voice dropping to a husky whisper. "Your belly growing rounder every day, your breasts heavy with milk." He leaned closer, folding her body further, his lips brushing her ear. "And I won't stop fucking you — not for one single day. I'll take you like this even when you're eight months along, your belly massive between us."

"Oh god, Keith," Sam gasped, her inner walls beginning to flutter again.

"I'll bend you over the kitchen counter, the bathroom sink," he panted, his thrusts becoming erratic, "I'll make you cum every day of your pregnancy, watch you waddle to our bed begging for my cock." His eyes blazed with desire. "And after those babies are born, I'll fill you again, keep you pregnant for years — our own perfect family bred from my cum deep inside you."

The taboo fantasy pushed Sam over the edge. Her second orgasm crashed through her with even greater force than the first, her body convulsing wildly beneath him. "Yes! Make me pregnant! Fill me with your babies!"

Keith roared as her pulsing walls triggered his

own release. He slammed into her one final time, grinding against her cervix as his cock swelled impossibly larger. "Take it all," he groaned. "Every. Last. Drop."

Sam felt the hot rush of his release flooding her deepest recesses, the volume still so astonishingly abundant, even after all these months. The sensation of being so thoroughly filled prolonged her orgasm, making her sob with pleasure as Keith continued to pump into her with small, grinding thrusts.

When the intense waves finally subsided, Keith carefully unwound her legs from around his neck, massaging her thighs as he helped her straighten them. He remained inside her, both of them savoring the connection as their breathing gradually steadied.

"That was ..." Sam whispered, unable to find adequate words.

Keith kissed her tenderly, a stark contrast to their animalistic coupling moments before. "I know." He stroked her hair back from her flushed face. "I love you, Sam."

"I love you, too." She looked up at him through the curtain of hair stuck to her sweaty forehead, and smirked. "Wanna go again?"

Keith chuckled, moving around ever so slowly inside her. "The body and spirit are willing, but ... the staff is getting pretty irked about my taking extended lunches every day." He kissed her, a quick peck on the tip of her nose. "Tonight, I promise — we'll fuck over and over again until we drop from exhaustion.

Sam smiled at the thought. "I'll hold you to that, mister."

Keith laughed, thrust into her one final time for good measure, then pulled out and crawled off the bed to get dressed. "Gotta go."

Sam lingered in bed after Keith had gone, feeling the warm wetness between her thighs. She stretched languorously, cat-like, savoring the pleasant ache that radiated through her well-used body. Keith's scent still clung to the sheets, a musky reminder of their passionate lunchtime tryst.

"Don't drip on the comforter," she reminded herself, carefully swinging her legs over the edge of the bed. She walked with deliberate steps toward the bathroom, feeling rivulets of Keith's abundant release threatening to escape down her inner thighs.

In the bathroom, she settled onto the toilet, letting gravity do its work. As she sat there, her gaze drifted to the cabinet beneath the sink where, all those months ago, she had hidden a small pink box — back when she had worried she was pregnant with Ty's baby.

On a whim, she reached down to open the cabinet.

Sam followed the instructions, then set the plastic stick on the counter. She washed her hands at a more relaxed pace than usual, then ... when the time was right, she picked up the test stick.

Her breath caught in her throat as she registered the two distinct pink lines.

Tears welled in her eyes as she pressed a trembling

hand to her flat abdomen. Somewhere inside her, a new life was forming.

Her heart filled with joy ... but she could not deny that her nipples also tightened against her thin nightgown, her inner muscles clenching in anticipation of many pleasures to come.

About the Author

Juliet McDuff is a lover of all things erotica; she is also the proverbial "crazy cat lady." She has written many erotic stories and shared them online, but *Blue is the Color of Seduction* is her first published novel. Ms. McDuff lives near Palm Springs, CA.